<u>Stick N Move II</u>

A novel

By
Shawn Black

RJ Publications, LLC

Newark, New Jersey

The characters and events in this book are fictitious. Any resemblance to actual persons, living or dead is purely coincidental.

RJ Publications
Kbwell02@yahoo.com
www.rjpublications.com
Copyright © 2009 by Shawn Black
All Rights Reserved
ISBN 978-0978637385

Printed in Canada

April 2009

1-2-3-4-5-6-7-8-9-10-

Acknowledgement

First I would like to thank God. Honestly, during the process of writing this novel, there were many times I wanted to quit. It was frustrating, I didn't have the support I thought I deserved and lots of things were simply not in my favor. I felt as if no one truly cared about what I was trying to do. Therefore, I took my problems to God.

After weeks of struggling to get people to do things I felt was important, I learned that no one person is going to put forth the needed energy in a project that's not their own. I realized that no one was going to chase my dream like me, and if I'm going to achieve any success and gratification from it, I needed to stop feeling sorry for myself and go hard, despite the difficulties that seemed to impede my progress. That said, I would like to thank the people who supported me through the beginning of my career as an author, and the new individuals/friends that have contributed to the completion of 'Product of Society."

My friend and Typist/Entrepreneur, Yolander Boston, thanks for lending an ear, and for the encouragement to continue pursuing my dreams. I also would like to thank Richard Jeanty, my publisher, for having patience.

I would like to thank Sheri Heastie for her tremendous help with the website, and undying friendship. David Gainer, my boy, my friend, my ace --

you stand alone, my brotha. Thank you for everything you've done and are doing for me. Tonnie Guerro, I appreciate everything you've done. And to my little cousin, Anlka Davis, I apologize for not adding you in my last book, so I made sure not to forget this time. Thanks for supporting me, and I love you. To my beautiful daughter Asia, and my handsome son, Devon, know that Daddy will be home SOON! I'm gonna do everything in my power to assure that you have a brighter future. To my beautiful niece, Zaria, Uncle Sean's going to spoil you right along with Asia, and thanks for riding with me.

My mother and sister, Katisha Blackwell and Gloria Davis, thanks for your undying support over these last eight plus years. To my brother, Ced, you already know what it is. But, I'll say it anyway. Thanks for everything; the visits, the convo, the money, and for holding your little brother down.

Temeka Mebane and Mrs. Sharon Walker, thanks for being a special part of my life. It feels good knowing I can turn to either of you for help, or just to hear inspiring words. I love both of you.

To the entire extended Davis, Graham and Walker family, thanks for your support. I can't forget my Scranton, South Carolina homegirl, Elaine Jones -- thank you for supporting me. Ronald Graham, "Big Herdie," you held your cuz down. Thanks a million, cuz.

Special shout outs to: Mona Gary, Terrance Blige, Torrance Jones aka J'Ville, Ronnie "Pillow Head" Dawson, Sexy Boss Lady, C. Williams, Roger Spicer, Eric Cowling, Kim Simpson, Lynn McCrary, aka Mistress Ghost Writer, Alfa Breed, my boy, Voll Greene, Dre Richardson, James Harris,, aka Six, James Sawyer, aka- J.J., Mr. James O. Ogle – Author of "Political Proverbs" and "Lynched At Law", Ramono Scott. To my Bronx NY crew: Sequoyah, aka Nikko and Sydney Scales,aka Mo' Black of Full Throttle ENT/PUB, my main man Harlem, A. Gortman, aka Corey. My crew from home - Tres-Four, Winston-Salem, Mike Hollister, my main nucca – Ahm T. from Pollock Town (Killa Camden) Pimps up Ho's down, James Hairston, Spodie, Donald Fields – Brick City, My Chicago Crew: Keith Lockhart, aka Chi Town's Finest, The Ohio Players; Eugene Evans, aka Soup, Carl Drewer, aka C note, Terrance "Buggzy" Tarver, Mr. "Cool Hand" Burroughs. My Virginia Crew: Shaun "Maestro" Swinson, Shawn Starling "the next hot author, Kevin Fuell, Jeff Williamson, aka, Nasty, Mike Stovall.   To my Pennsylvania Crew: Thomas Williams, aka, "Poppa" author of "GREED", "ENVY" and "DECEIT", I'll be 'lookin to cop that hot joint. My good friends, Jacob Chudzinski and Manish Patel – super thanks! And lastly, to my B'More and D.C. Crew: Twan Mason, Poop, Charles Aaron Green, William Ferrell – next hot author in line, and Robert Thomas, aka Cheese. Shout out to my ATL homie – Dwayne Turner, author of "Hurricane Atlanta. Sherwok Lewis and Anthony "Honeybun" Cameron. To my Georgia Crew Chico Baldwin and Earl Howard, I appreciate you. To my boy Steve Salter, CEO of M.O.B. Clothing, I'm waiting for some hot fashions.

To my fans and readers, thank you most of all for your support. I will always try to give you a story that will touch the fabric of things we possess. For both Yasmina and Serosa, we all have family and friends, which we can relate to when it comes to these experiences. Thank You.

Product of Society
"Survival at Any Cost"

Part One

Chapter 1
Freedom

"Whew!" Serosa sighed, inhaling a deep breath of fresh air. Her grateful lungs instantly felt the difference from the stale processed air she'd breathed the last 365 days, 3 hours, 12 minutes and 20 seconds inside the prison.

Glancing over her shoulder, Serosa looked back at the huge draconian structure and shook her head with relief. "I'm finally out this bitch!"

Having survived the past nine years, moving from foster home to county ward, to completing her tenth year in prison, the euphoria of being free was overwhelming as she anxiously waited with nowhere to go. From where she stood, it was hard to grasp the things she had once taken for granted.

"The sun," she mouthed, looking directly at the early morning rays. "It even shines brighter on the outside. Damn!" She cursed, her gaze leading her around the expansive parking lot of the establishment that housed her for the last year. "I'm never risking my freedom again, over some bullshit."

Her thoughts trailed off when the hissing of an airplane flew overhead. With her belongings packed tightly into a small laundry bag, she waited patiently, the prospects of her destination, uncertain. In the back of her mind, a hint of sadness engulfed her, realizing there was no one to come home to. No family, no friends, just Serosa. Thinking about it, that's how her troubles began.

****

"Anthony, Scorcher, whatever it is they call you!" Agent Vincent yelled over the desperate cries of people caught in the crossfire. He realized his supervisor, chief Sculea, was about to start an all out war.

"Look," he pleaded, "just drop your weapons, man, it doesn't have to end this way."

Fearing the worst, the agent's main concerns were the innocent bystanders. Two females haphazardly ran directly into the arms of Scorcher and Murray. Hidden behind Yasmina, Serosa frighteningly gripped her legs. Her father was about to squeeze the trigger, taking the lives of the women and officer, as he trained the huge black weapon from side to side.

At the time, she was young, not old enough to really comprehend why this was happening, but wise enough to know when danger was present. She tugged and jerked viciously at Yasmina's clothing.

Angry agents sat perched atop roofs of cars and in between trucks. Others crouched on the ground, within inches of the fugitives trapped in the parking lot, adrenaline-hyped fingers itching to squeeze the trigger. Scorcher; his eyes reading bloody murder, gruffed another demand, still not getting the agents' response to his first one.

"Me tell ya again, Mon. Let me family leave and everyting will be alright."   In the following minutes, an eerie quietness surrounded the frenzied area. Then from nowhere, came the voice.

Looking back on it, Serosa understood what her parents were doing on that fateful day as everyone listened in hopes that Scorcher would comply, and not create a bloodbath.

The Feds, after having finally caught up with Yasmina, viewed her as a menace to society. She'd participated in murder and drug dealings and they had stopped at nothing to see that she was apprehended or killed. It was her charismatic incantations that stunned everyone around the parking lot that day, causing them to lower their guards a second too long.

The agents were poised, ready for the command to fire at will. One officer, a young-dark haired Caucasian rookie, prayed silently that Scorcher listened to Yasmina. He wanted to enjoy another night with his wife and two daughters. But, his dreams were abruptly shattered when Yasmina seized the opportunity, grabbing hold of his weapon.

The barrage of gunfire seemed to last forever. Metal was pierced as bullets slammed into vehicles. Glass shards flew from busted windows. Terrifying screams erupted throughout the crowd. What remained, as the smoke cleared, was a bloodbath of bodies littering the parking lot. Frozen from fear, Serosa stood with her hands covering her eyes and ears. But, it was that one familiar woeful sob that stood out. Her mother's body shook uncontrollably over the bullet-riddled body of her father, Scorcher.

Afraid and now crying herself, she ran full speed toward the only two people she loved, only to be swept up in the arms of an angry agent. This would be the last time she'd see either of her parents. And now, as she stood undecided about her future, the memories of the pain she'd had to endure since then, brought on events that began as a nightmare. One she would never forget.

Chapter 2
Memories....Pain

Serosa's heart pounded through the thin fabric of her worn and tattered shirt. All sorts of thoughts raced through her mind. "Are they going to electrocute me, again? Why?"

Those fears manifested deeper as she lay outstretched on her back, atop the gurney. In her consternation, Serosa sought for understanding as to why this was happening to her. "If my parents were here to tell me it would be alright, maybe I could go through this," she reasoned. However, having gone through this before, she quickly realized that her knights in shining armor weren't going to rescue her anytime soon.

The tightening cinch of the leather straps being fastened around her ankle and wrist reminded her of what was to come next. One by one, a different physician filed in, attaching a device to her body. From past experience, she knew that fighting would only make things worse. And surrendering to tears wouldn't win the affection of the maniacs before her. Quietly, she surrendered, realizing the pain would end only when they felt she had suffered enough or gave up the information they obsessively tried to force out of her.

"Okay, my dear," drooled the voice of an elderly white male standing above her. He wore a white lab jacket and a stethoscope wrapped around his neck where a tie once was.

In Serosa's mind, the gentleman peering down at her could fool anyone who was naïve. With his slow gait, wrinkled skin and the ease in which he spoke, she knew his disguise probably lured many into the trap, which they called the "St.-Boneventures Girl Reform School." Surely, this man was not to be trusted, including the other nameless faces in the room, especially the gentleman standing behind the doctor, who was probably a Senator. The fear was clearly etched on Serosa's face as she listened to the two speak of things she wasn't familiar with. Then without warning, the older man, whose name was Dr. Carmichael, according to the Senator-looking guy, started to unbutton her blouse.

"We're going to administer a series of test on you, my dear," he stated in his shaky voice. "We just want to learn the behaviors of black children your age, to see what makes you so aggressive." A tear creased the corner of her eye as she thought back to the same test taken a year earlier. She knew what to expect next - pain.

For what seemed like days, which were in fact hours, Serosa endured her torture. The agony of being prodded with instruments, shocked by machines, and poked with needles left her dazed, confused, and in terrible pain. Repeatedly, she was questioned about her childhood, the one she vaguely remembered. However, she managed to remain strong, refusing to let her captors break her spirit.

At one point during the session, Serosa strived to imagine what it would be like if her parents were alive. This helped block the pain, but the questions kept coming.

"Serosa," chimed another physician, this one was much younger than the other one, "I have a daughter around your age. Her name is Brittany. She's nine also." The physician used this approach thinking it would make her more comfortable. It was an approach he'd learned years back in a parenting class. Continuing, he added, "My daughter, she loves her mother and we try to give her everything a kid her age needs. Is that what your parents were like?"

Seconds elapsed and Serosa stared unblinkingly at the man. "This lame man think I'm gon' fall for that one?" she conceded in her thoughts, not bothering to answer. She abruptly turned away from his gaze, focusing her eyes on the others around the room occupied by their expensive equipment. A thought occurred, which brought a smile to her lips. Something she'd learned years ago after her first analysis. But, the young physician caught the slight flicker of happiness, and queried, "Is there something amusing about the questions I ask?" he hissed, exposing an unpleasant scowl.

Henry's questioning fell upon deaf ears. Serosa was in another world, in a time and place where nothing but happy moments existed. She was at her fifth birthday party. She was a princess, admiring the diamond-encrusted bracelet with her initials inscribed on it.

"Once again," Henry admonished, shaking Serosa out of her stupor. "I'm asking you what is so funny?" Henry had been with the St. Bonaventures Program for eight years. Before, he was employed with Social Services, helping at-risk-youth, until allegations of sexual abuse with a minor surfaced. Now, hired as an intern, he worked under the watchful eye of Dr. Carmichael.

The insults coming from the young girl lying before him was too much. Henry slammed his notepad against the table. If not for the loud beeping and chirping noises of the machines, everyone present would have realized how angry he actually was.

A menacing stare, followed by, "Okay, if you want it that way!" told Serosa that she was in danger. However, her attempt to warn the others was futile.

Casting a quick glance over his shoulder, Henry fished a syringe from the pocket of his lapel. With a hand covering Serosa's mouth, he fed the substance into her veins, slowly. As she lay beneath the powerful grip of the physician, she quivered. The substance flowing through her veins felt like hot grease. The more she fought, the quicker the liquid spread. The pain was intense. So intense, her eyes teetered on the brink of rolling back in her head. Fear gripped her. At no other time during the course of her tests had this method been used. Understanding the length that this new physician would go to retrieve information, she realized it was best to tell him what he wanted to hear.

Fighting desperately to get back to that moment of happiness, Serosa quickly realized it wasn't going to happen and a soft, muffled groan escaped her mouth. Henry removed his hand. His ear mere inches away from her lips.

"Oh!" the little bitch wants to talk now, huh?" his words were laced with venom as he teased her. "Well," he continued, "Maybe you will answer my questions the next time I ask?" He waited, receiving a slow nod from Serosa.

After reaching an agreement, Henry removed his hand. A few questions more followed about her parents. The success he was having with Serosa was the most anyone in the facility had ever obtained, including, Dr. Carmichael. And for a child as young as she was to have taken the life of another child her age, Henry knew this could be a prodigious career move.

His questioning continued. One after another, he shot Serosa a question. In return, she didn't hesitate to answer. She spoke freely about the private school in Hawaii, her huge room, Murray and Felecia, the music studio where her father's rap and reggae was created. She even relayed witnessing the gruesome scene the day her father was killed in the parking lot, and police whisked her mother away.

From the moment the first words left Serosa's mouth, machines across the room erratically beeped. In unison, heads turned towards Serosa and Henry.

Dr. Carmichael, the Senator, and a host of observing physicians watched feverishly, eagerly scribbling on their pads as Henry continued with his macabre show.

"Now, Serosa," he said, this time a benign mask of kindness to his voice.

"You were saying that your mother, Yasmina and father, Scorcher, were good parents." He didn't wait for a response.

"How could that be? I mean, they sold drugs and murdered innocent people. Would you say that you inherited their traits? I mean, you killed your roommate." Everyone held their breath.

The inexplicable rustle of Serosa's body twitching underneath the constraints could be heard. More than that, the many who observed her noted the piercing loneliness in her eyes. And the obvious was certain to Serosa, she would never ever see her parents again, no matter how much those people questioned her. One fact remained as she lay before the physicians; she was being tortured for something she had nothing to do with, mostly because she was available.

Her eyes darting back and forth from one individual to the other, Serosa thought about what she really wanted to say. Again, Henry quipped, "Serosa, we're waiting."

She exhaled a sigh. Fixing her mouth that now tasted of cotton, she said,

"I don't care how many more times you stick me with needles, fondle my vagina…" her last words caused a startled gasp to escape everyone's mouth. Their eyes landed on Henry. Serosa continued.

"Or, pretend to be trying to help me." Her eyes roamed each person. "In my nine years, I've endured more, and witnessed more than you can imagine. My daddy was killed by people like you, momma is waiting to be killed by people like you, and for the last three years I've been experimented on by people like you, and you expect me to tell you about my parents."

The room went silent. Not one word was uttered. Listening to the onslaught of words coming from the child left everyone in awe. They knew it was virtually impossible for someone so young to be that articulate. Henry anxiously fiddled with his pockets, searching endlessly for the syringe he'd managed to hide from himself.

"It has to be here," he groped his body nervously. "I have to sedate this bitch before she ruins me."

After finding the syringe and filling it with a different serum, he injected Serosa. She was nearing the end of her spiel.

"… Then you trap us with your so called laws. Laws that were intended for blacks. And here I am, a child, nine years old, being tortured. Just yesterday Henry wanted to treat me like a..a..l.la.lady. Coming to my room ex..expos..ing his self." Her eyelids fluttered. Everyone gazed holes into Henry.

"T.ttell em'. Ain't dat' r.rr.ight, Henry?"

Henry shifted nervously. Sweat trickled down his face. Looking to everyone, he pleaded with his hands for some sort of trust.

"…I mean, come on guys. Who are you going to believe, me or her?" He said sheepishly. "For Christ's sake, she's under heavy sedatives. No one could think straight under that much medicine."

Serosa didn't give up. The more the serum worked her, the harder she fought.

"Y.ya..you people have t..taken everythi..nng from me. My mother… my father …th..tha..they dead." The medicine was rocking her to sleep.

No one could muster a word. Some were in tears, others confused. They all listened.

"There's n.n..no one left for me. I.I'm pr..product of soc..ciet..y." Her world went dark.

Chapter 3
Prison...Life

"Zone 1-Gate B, Alpha House," the medium female guard announced as she pressed the hand-held radio.

The noise level was deafening. Within the three levels of tiers, confetti and all sorts of debris showered the floor including, paper, books and tissue. It was Serosa's homecoming. When first hearing of the young star, in the eyes of most female inmates serving time at Prag, she was somewhat of a legend. Not too many child murderers got the attention Serosa did. In this regard, many salivated at the mere thought of Serosa being transferred to Prag. They had followed her life since day one.

Now as the corrections officer, Serosa and the other new arrival, Trish, awaited entry, the rattling of metal against bars and blasphemous yells of threats and insults, told of the welcoming party. Danger!

Alpha House was filthy. A bunch of row house units aligned in columns, facing each other. The place was once an 18th Century dungeon, one of the oldest standing buildings in the state of Maryland. The unmistaken scent of urine, feces, blood and death wafted throughout the place. The stench caused Serosa to dry heave. The pungent odor of fear was also recognizable. And each inmate standing and peeking through the slit in the bars could smell where the stench resonated.

Most of the inmates were there for long stints. Their crimes ranged from double murder, triple homicides, to simple larceny. Sentences were varied and ranged from one year to (LWOP) Life Without the Possibility of Parole. And to watch Serosa try to mask her fear by wearing a malicious grimace, most thought it funny.

Staring throughout the bars of the door, Serosa watched as rodents scampered across the floor. Just above her head, water leaked, leaving an iridescent, muddy puddle at her feet. She felt the tension. The atmosphere radiated too much for it to go unnoticed.

The doors finally opened, and the chains churning against the metal emitted a sound like a draw bridge opening. The CO, Benita, offered a few last words of advice.

"Ladies," she screamed above the noise, "In time you will come to know me as a pretty descent person." Eyeing Serosa, she added. "In here, there are only wolves preying on who they can find weakness in, no one is to be trusted." Turning briefly to Trish, then back to Serosa, she added. "I normally don't go out of my way when it comes to giving advice, but you two are still merely babies." Sliding an unnoticed hand between Serosa's line, Benita finished.

"I couldn't live with myself if something happened to either of you. Just know that you have an angel up above watching over you, so be careful, your name is floating like you're a celebrity.

At the lady's last words, Serosa questioned her with her bewildered eyes. She knew all too well the dangers she faced. And she was prepared, at least she thought. Her thoughts trailed off when hearing the monstrous door clank shut.

Entering an environment far different from the one they were used to, each took cautious steps. The corridor was even louder now that they were inside. Trish was the first to falter. She shook uncontrollably, and each inmate watching sized up their mark. Each time a hand extended from within a cell bar, she froze in her steps. Insults were the same. Each time one came her way, she flinched. Serosa remained unphased. Her facial expression was unreadable and her steps, unstoppable.

Making it halfway down the long corridor, which seem to Trish like walking the "Green Mile," mirror after mirror after mirror appeared. Then, the first encounter.

The woman towered, standing at the bars, her large hands gripping each cylindrical steel beam. All 6 feet 2 inches of her massive frame occupied the cell. With a scar running the length of her face, she stared unbendingly at Trish, who cowered further to the tables in the center of the floor. It was the woman's salacious introduction that caught Trish and Serosa off guard.

"Hey, babies," she smiled, her molten black eyes reading sinister. "If you girls need anything, you call Sherry."

Sherry's hospitality was followed with a lustful lick of her areola, while her free hand lightly abraded her unzipped trousers.

Benita interjected after seeing this, "That's enough, Sherry. If anything happens to either of these ladies, I'm personally holding you responsible. And you know what that means!"

Sherry seethed.   She knew that CO's like Benita and others used the hole as a way to control inmates.   But, another thing Sherry realized, the hole at Prag was unlike any other she'd been to during her stint in prison.   And this brought back memories of why she hated it so much.

****

Eighteen-year-old Sherida was shuttled from prison to prison. Although she was on the yard in front of hundreds of inmates who preyed on people like her, she went about her tasks.   The itch was driving her crazy, and the only way to stop it was to fix it. Heroin! Sherida hadn't been on the compound for a month before finding trouble.   After becoming heavily indebted to a Mexican Syndicate known as "Los Nuestras," word had spread that her death was on the horizon. Sherry pounced on the opportunity.

For her, it was a sure way to claim a prize she'd wanted from the first time she laid eyes on Sherida.   But, over time, things began to decline drastically, after Sherry learned that Sherida had been seeing another young beauty on the compound. Though the relationship was new, Sherry couldn't tolerate being made a fool of. Not with the reputation she held in prison.

Late one night, the guards made their midnight rounds, allowing Sherry time to produce a small bag for Sherida.   Sherry watched as blood mixed with water and the substance flowed inside the clear syringe. She counted seconds as the heroin flowed through Sherida's veins.

The entire week, Sherry debated numerous ways to handle her problems. One day, while working in the kitchen, it came to her.

Sherida's naked body jerked viciously, convulsing with vicious spasms. Her eyes puffy, red and swollen, honed in on Sherry long enough to see the snide smile formed across her lips.

The deceit was obvious. Sherry made no move to help Sherida who fought with everything she had to get to her feet. A time or two, Sherry shoved Sherida to the bed.

The poison was slowly staking its claim. Sherida clawed at the bed sheets, flinging them to the floor. After grabbing hold of the bar, she finally made it to her feet. The veins pulsated throughout her body, varicose and blue. Her forehead, neck, arms, and breasts, all contained the tattoo of death floating through her body.

Clutching at her throat, she gasped for air, her light-brown hue turning a purplish-blue by the second. Her legs wobbled. They clapped together. But, it was the blood secretion from her nails that spoke of the Grim Reaper's arrival. Within seconds, she was dead.

An investigation was launched, landing Sherry in the hole for nine months. Though she beat the case, having been cleared of all charges for lack of evidence, the memory of her long stay remained fresh on her mind.

Never again did she want to suffer at the hands of the Extraction Team, who unmercifully pumped keg after keg of mace in her cell everyday, refused her of showers, recreation, meals, and administered fierce beatings with nightsticks.

Now, as Sherry listened to the other inmates laugh and make jokes about the hole, she slowly sauntered back to her cot, her mind beginning to conceive a new plan.

****

Benita had gained control. But deep down, she knew how easily it could've gotten out of hand. Making it to their cell, Trish coddled her belongings to her chest. Just as Benita radioed for the door to open, a scream reverberated throughout the hall. The sound was bone chilling, and everyone knew where it came from. Even Benita tensed at finding the woman's hand reaching for Serosa. However, it was her words that sent shivers down Benita's spine.

"Deena, I thought you were dead. I . . I . . . killed you."

DANGER

"We interrupt this program for some breaking news!" said the thin-framed brown-skinned female cradling the microphone to her mouth. Surrounded by a crew of media personnel, they stood in front of the huge prison that was surrounded by a 40ft cement wall, rows of razor wire sitting at the base of it. Pointing, she spoke with urgency in her voice.

"Sometime this morning, authorities confirmed that an inmate waiting to be transferred from here," she pointed at a sign that read, "The Federal

Penitentiary ADX, here in Amarillo, Texas, has escaped. The inmate was headed for a Federal Death Row Facility at an undisclosed location. It is unknown how the escapee named, Osei Love, managed to break out of one of the nation's most secured prisons, but there are speculations of possible help from the inside. At this time, authorities are asking that you keep all doors locked, windows checked, and don't, I reiterate, don't hesitate to call the nearest police station if you see this man. Do not attempt to apprehend him yourself. He's extremely dangerous. I'm Wanda Sellers, reporting live, News Channel 2."

Chapter 4
New Beginnings

"Rochelle speaking," Damita answered, suspicious of just about anyone who called her number. Although the brunt of ten years had elapsed, she was still apprehensive about the past life she'd led.

It started with the move to Seattle, WA. Wanting a fresh start at life, something that both she and her boys Jaime and Derek, could enjoy, Damita gathered the money she made hustling, and never looked back. But, there was one person who would forever remain a fixture in her life, Yasmina. It was during a visit, the first year of Yasmina's incarceration, that a bombshell would be dropped on her, changing Damita's life forever.

"Listen to me," Yasmina said, in a serious tone and expression. For the past six months, she had experienced a wave of emotions trying to adjust to her new life. The loss of the only man she'd ever loved other than her father, the separation from her only daughter, as well as sitting on Death Row, wasn't something she could easily shake from her mind.

Knowing that in order for Serosa to have a future, a chance at life, there would be things she needed. Knowing the only person who never turned her back on her, the one person she trusted with her life, Yasmina required Damita's undivided attention.

A quick glance at the surveillance camera mounted overhead, she began speaking in code.

"These people here are going at full speed to assure that my death sentence sticks. The lawyer says there may be a chance, a slim one that he could get me a stay. And this will allow him more time to gather evidence." Yasmina was about to continue when she noticed the confused look on Damita's face.

The entire time Yasmina spoke, Damita wondered where she was heading. She knew what the attorney was trying to do. She was the one who hired him. However, just as she was about to protest, Yasmina placed a finger in the air.

"Let me finish, then you'll understand." She sighed audibly, "You know you gon' need someone to watch over and take care of my baby, right?"

Damita shook her head

Continuing, Yasmina smiled. "We had some good times, didn't we? I mean, who would've thought that a bunch of girls from the hood calling themselves the PLATINUM CHICKS could've taken a game like that by storm." A slight chuckle escaped Damita's mouth.

"But like I was saying, "Yasmina added. "When Scorcher purchased our home in the Groves, I swore to never leave that place. It was beautiful. And the gazebo, my favorite relaxation spot of the entire house, I remember days when I escaped there for peace of mind. I could hide easily, and no one would ever think to look for me out there." An alarm rang in Damita's head.

"I wonder if it's still standing." Yasmina finished.

Once the last few words were spoken Damita eyed Yasmina knowingly.

It only took a few days for Damita to make it back to Florida, a place she vowed to never step foot in ever again.

The home, still holding its illustrious beauty from a distance, was definitely startling for Damita as she got closer. Tall weeds, brush, vines covering the window, termites, had all taken refuge at the place. Slowly, she cautiously made an entrance through a splintered door that hung on a hinge. The interior was dark with only a sliver of light beaming from a hole of a two-by-four used as a window guard.

Eeriness crept over her. It wasn't the cat she watched scamper across the threshold of the room the second she stepped foot inside the place. Damita felt the presence of someone watching her. Having adjusted her eyes to the impenetrable darkness, the dank smell of mold drifted into Damita's nose. She noticed the furniture; leather sofa ripped to shreds with the material inside soaking from months of rain and the china cabinet, a family heirloom – with the windows broken and shattered. Stepping over a shattered vase, Damita followed a single beam of light. It led to the kitchen. With no patience, only wanting to see if she could in fact find what she had come for, Damita unyieldingly focused on getting through the boarded up back door, and to the gazebo.

For seconds, she stood gazing the huge structure. In her mind, she could now understand why the place could offer such solace. It was a retreat. Instantly, Damita transformed her thoughts. "If I wanted to hide something from everyone, where would I put it?" Her thoughts went back to the conversation with Yasmina in the visiting room.

In the corner sat an old wicker chair. Realizing that the cushion on the chair was worn, a smile appeared on Damita's face. "Bingo!"

After taking a quick survey of her surroundings, she made her way to the entrance. The skylight was still intact. At first, Damita was about to shun the notion of something being hidden there. There was only clear plastic paneling. Then, she noticed a small lever protruding from a far corner. Moving the chair to the center of the floor, she stepped atop the seat, turned the twisted bar, and watched as the panels parted. Carefully, she ran her finger along a groove of about two inches. Just as she was about to discard the notion, her nail brushed against something. Buried deep, wrapped within a dusty cloth surrounded by plastic, was a thick-folded piece of paper. Once again, Damita peered her head through the door. The coast was clear. Unraveling the contents, she was shocked to find the numbers and pass codes to accounts overseas, in the Bahamas.

****

With her thoughts on her life, which had suddenly taken a drastic turn for the better, Damita couldn't shake the thought the startling news received from her boys, Derek and Jamie, one day as she helped with their school work. Nine hours and twenty-three minutes later, her car drove into the City of Portland, Oregon and it was where she would begin a new life.

But now, as she listened to the caller on the other end to speak, a grave expression covered her face. "How did he get this number?" she whispered, running to her window, looking out. Assuring that the locks on her doors were set, Damita made a beeline for the 52' Plasma Screen mounted on the wall. Pressing the menu button, she scrolled through the display until she came to last caller. Fear and panic gripped her when her eyes read, "UNIDENTIFIED CALLER".

Chapter 5
Desperate Measures

After ensuring the safety of Serosa to her cell, Benita inconspicuously made her way into the library. The room was small and cramped. Removing the thin razor from inside her trouser pocket, she inched well into a corner beneath an old air duct. Her heart pounded noisily. She couldn't believe that after twenty years of working at the facility, a faithful employee who never once called in sick or missed a day's work would have to resort to breaking the law. But, desperation had long set in, and if becoming a criminal was the only way to assuage Chaunna's chances at the life threatening disease, Benita vowed to do it again, if it came to that.

As she dialed the numbers, her thoughts lumbered back to when she was approached with the dangerous proposition.

+++++

Benita punched in exactly at 7:00 a.m., though she wasn't too eager to start the day. Earlier in the month, her daughter, Chaunna, the apple of her eye, was diagnosed with Acute Lymphoblast Leukemia. And having to watch a once healthy sixteen-year-old reduced to being bedridden was taking its toll on her.

After utilizing all of her resources, realizing that she still wouldn't be able to afford the best health care coverage for the type of surgery Chaunna needed, she scraped up what money she had left, and boarded a plane to Portland.

Unaware of how loud she was, Damita sat mumbling to herself. She was too consumed and too distraught over learning that Yasmina's first Stay of Execution had been denied. Grabbing her I-Phone from her bag, she strolled through her itinerary checking proposed dates for future hair shows. Since receiving the money and accounts from Yasmina, Damita invested wisely. A day spa, an exotic car salon, and a chain of hair salons throughout different cities that hosted hair shows. Damita's reputation for hosting shows such as Bronner Bros in Atlanta, catapulted her into the majors. Benita was sitting with Chaunna posted in a wheelchair beside her while listening to the woman mumble incoherently to herself about a Stay being denied. She surmised Damita was sympathizing over her boyfriend.

Adjusting the carry-on bag sitting atop her lap, Benita leaned over and tugged at Damita's sleeve. "Excuse me, miss?" she stated politely.

Damita's stare was uninviting.

"Yes," she answered in a dry tone.

After sliding Chaunna's wheelchair closer, Benita introduced herself.

"...and this is my daughter, Chaunna." She smiled, extending a hand.

After introductions were exchanged, she continued,

"I wasn't being nosey, but I overheard you mention something about a Stay of Execution being denied."

Damita wearily eyed Benita.

The fact that this woman was eavesdropping didn't sit well with her, but she could sense genuineness in the woman's questioning.

Shaking her head rather than mouthing anything, Damita awaited more conversation. For a moment, nothing was said.

Benita was silently doing an assessment of the stranger she willingly approached in conversation. Her surmise led her to believe that Damita was a college student. She looked to be no more than twenty-five, and her clothing read Hip Hop Couture. But there's also something about her she couldn't put a finger on. She was sophisticated. Benita thought, just as Damita said, "And what was it about my conversation that intrigued you?"

Embarrassed, and caught off guard by the remark, Benita smirked.

"Forgive me for being so rude, but," she moved closer. "I work in a prison, and maybe I could lend a little advice, or at least, point you to someone who could help with your situation."

For seconds there was silence and then a smile.

The brief and coincidental encounter between the two opened up doors that neither thought possible. And for Damita, she'd learned that Benita worked at the same prison Serosa was housed. This led to more conversation, and Damita learned of the crisis Benita faced with Chaunna's medical costs. With no money or coverage, she risked losing her daughter forever.

That day the two walked away feeling optimistic. On one hand, Damita could rest assured knowing Serosa had someone watching over her. On the other, Benita knew if this trip didn't turn out the way she desperately hoped it did, there was another option. Damita!

Chapter 6
Conspiratorial

"Ah, yes, I totally agree, Sir." stammered, Dr. Carmichael, who tried his damnest to explain things to his boss. Continuing, he added, "But, our main objective at the facility is learning the behaviors of the young ladies, and quite frankly, I think she was as normal as any ch....:"

The doctor's words were lost in a barrage of insults that followed.

"You imbecile," barked the caller, causing Dr. Carmichael to jerk nervously. His face was beet red from embarrassment as he placed the receiver back to his ear.

The lecture continued.

"You... You think I give a damn abut what you think? I know what our objectives are at that God-forsaken place." Pausing momentarily, the caller added, "Have you suddenly forgotten, I'm the reason for your employment?"

Dr. Carmichael remained silent while the caller continued, "Now, I want you to get your head out of your ass and find that file. And doctor, might I add that it would be in your best interest that the young lady never leaves Prag alive. Do you understand what I'm saying, doctor?" The line went dead.

Dr. Carmichael, hands shaking terribly, doodled with the computer's mouse. Vigorously, he searched every program. "Damn it!" He cursed, not finding the file. "Where could it be?" he questioned himself.

In the subsequent silence that followed, he thought of every excuse he could give his employer. Anything, as long as it bought time, something he desperately needed at the moment.

An hour had passed and still no file. Nothing on the computer stated a file had once been stored. Confused by this sudden revelation, Dr. Carmichael uttered, "Who in their right mind would remove such a highly classified document without my authorization?"

He removed his glasses. Sweat droplets formed oily beads on his forehead. "What does Serosa's file from St. Bonaventure have to do with her leaving Prag, alive?"

There was no one to answer his thoughts, but what was certain was the tone of his employer's voice plagued him terribly.

Picking up the phone, Dr. Carmichael dialed a number, and waited.

A voice answered.

"Hello." It was Henry. Looking at the clock and realizing it read 1:00 in the morning, he angrily muttered, "This better be good."

Dr. Carmichael's voice was labored, but he was able to utter, "Umm, Henry…listen to me," before Henry went into a rage.

"For Christ's sake, Charles! It's one in the morning." He slid his glasses over his eyes.

Aware of the movement, Henry's wife Cary rolled over.

"Honey, is everything okay?"

By this time Henry had abandoned the bed and was wrapping his satin robe around his torso. Stepping into his bedroom shoes, he slipped into the hallway leaving Cary propped on her elbow.

In a low tone, he spoke trying not to disturb his sleeping daughter.

"Okay, Charles, now what's so important that you couldn't wait until morning?"

Dr. Carmichael didn't hesitate. He went straight to the point.

"How long have we known each other, Henry?"

"What?" Henry furrowed his brow." I...I don't understand, Charles."

"Damn it, Henry!" Dr. Carmichael cursed, clearly agitated. "How long have we known each other?" He asked, clearly upset.

This time Henry caught on.

"Since... since the company," he replied, still confused. "But, what does that have to do with anything...the reason you're calling me so early in the morning?"

Henry's reference to the company meant the C.I.A. Both he and Dr. Carmichael were associates, but were forced to retire because of a scandal within the government. Now employed by one of Washington D.C.'s most influential, they worked at St. Bonaventure Girls Reform School.

Dr. Carmichael still leaned before his computer.

"You do remember the girl, Serosa? The one we ran those series of tests on before she was transported to Prag?"

A hand pressed against his forehead, Henry thought, "How can I forget? That little bitch almost cost me everything… my job, my family."

"You're talking about the crazy girl who killed her roommate when she was seven? Yes, I remember her, but Charles, that was ten years ago."

Dr. Carmichael strenuously repressed the anger that had mounted. He had to remain cool. Not lose his temper. He was on borrowed time.

Finally, he asked. "The file, Henry, where is it?"

The tone sent chills down Henry's spine. He remembered a time when he and his mentor were alone in the lab and Dr. Carmichael questioned him about the implications Serosa made that day on the table.

As usual, Henry denied it. But, deep inside, his gut was telling him that his mentor didn't believe him, so he had to have assurance that anything about Serosa could never come back to haunt him. He removed the disc.

Appalled at the accusation, Henry said, "This could've waited until morning when we were back at work. For all I know, you're probably overlooking the file it's under. I'll talk with you tomo…"

Dr. Carmichael quickly interjected.

"But you don't understand, Henry. I need that if..."

Silence

Henry stared at his phone. He thought he had mistakenly pressed the button.

"Hello! Hello... Charles, are you there?"

Breathing.

A soft click. Then, a seemingly loud dial tone.

Dr. Carmichael stood just within the door of his chambers. He was unaware of the intruder who'd crossed the threshold of the hallway moments earlier.

As for the professional, he'd done this type of job numerous times. After listening, assuring that the doctor didn't have what he'd come for, the assassin quietly screwed the silencer. Having made sure that Dr. Carmichael's wife remained asleep, the assassin then stood within earshot of the doctor's back, shrouded in dark garb. Before Dr. Carmichael realized what happened, blood, tissue, and brain matter painted the wall and the computer.

The assassin walked over to the bloodied screen, wiping it, and the phone clear. The digital readout relayed the number 202-555-1967. 19 Weaver Place. He knew where to find the disc.

"Now, ain't dat' about a bitch!" Kasmir cursed, still upset about what he'd been through in court earlier. Twirling his fork through mushy spaghetti noodles, his mind was consumed with deep hatred for his ex. Letting out a deep belch from his mouth, Shukre said, "Yeah, and dem' bitch ass niggas are planning to testify against, Vick, too. That shit's fucked up!"

Kasmir cast a snide glance at Shukre. He snapped

"Dumb ass, nigga, I ain't talking about Michael Vick." Shukre was the one wearing the confused look now. Kasmir continued. "I'm talking about Jakita's bitch ass.

You see the smirk on her face when she left the courtroom?" He paused to see if anyone would reply, then added. "She knew she had me by the balls when the judge ordered me to pay $1,700 and gave her full custody of Kiara and Keon. Why is it that you pay for the child's clothing, feed the child, and you're in the child's life, but you still have to pay child support to some bitch that's only going to get her nails and hair done with the money?"

Again, his questions went unanswered.

While this heated one-sided conversation unfolded, Dalvin sat lost in his own world. He'd barely touched his plate. Though his thoughts were on something totally different at the moment, he wondered about the two homies that he kicked it with every day.

Since stepping out of prison, Dalvin narrowed the people down around him to only two, Kasmir and Shukre. Though they didn't visit him while he was on lock, they sent money whenever they could. This showed him a lot about the two. But with what was revealed to him by Damita, Dalvin realized that Kasmir and Shukre's hearts would be tested soon, and he knew from past experience, when trouble came knocking at your door, your true measure will reveal itself. This led back to a memory where he found out the true size of his own heart.

***

"Mr. Cowling!" Agent Vincent said with a smile on his face as he gestured for Dalvin to enter.

Upon realizing it was the same federal agents who had arrested him months before the Platinum Chicks took their fall, Dalvin sucked his teeth.

"And what pleasure do I owe the two of you, Andy Griffith and Barney Fife?"

The joke wasn't taken as implied.

Agent Wallace grabbed Dalvin roughly by the wrist and flung him over a chair.

"Sit!"

Dalvin felt like a nightmare had been rehashed. "What in the fuck could these clowns want with me?" He questioned himself as all sorts of things played in his mind. "Shit, they got me, and on a fresh ten while you 'trippin."

Pondering his own silent questioning, he was brought back to reality when Agent Vincent slid a chair next to his.

He straddled it.

"Now," he said, looking to his partner who opened a folder, "What's it gon' be?"

A smirk formed at Agent Wallace's mouth. "Yeah, Dalvin, my man," he slowly ambled over until he was beside, Dalvin. "We'll overlook the smart comment, besides, we're the ones who'll be going home to our wives… maybe get a shot of pussy, eat some real food, and sleep in a real bed."

The agent's subtle way of throwing insults worked. Dalvin seethed and his slouched body squirmed in his seat.

"Oh yeah," Dalvin quickly retorted. "Well, I won't be in here forever. I do have an out date."

Agent Vincent whistled in astonishment. "I guess you heard that, Scotty."

Agent Wallace didn't laugh. He was angry, upset, and tired of dealing with people like Dalvin.

"Anyways," he said, taking a shot at Dalvin. "We didn't come here to be entertained by your Def Comedy routine, or whatever it is you brothas call it. We came to offer you a deal."

Dalvin wrinkled his face.

"Like us brothas!" he shouted incredulously, and then continued. "My, man, I don't know what planet you come from, but the last time I checked, yo' mutha-fuckin' ass was just as black as I am. Look in the mirror, brotha!"

The embarrassed agent was about to protest when Dalvin interrupted.

"And I'm not interested in any fucking deals you clowns have to offer!"

Slamming the folder against the tabletop, Agent Wallace cursed.

"Damn it!" I'm tired of playing games with your black ass. You think we came all the way up here to kick it with you? Hell, no! We came to see if you would be smart, or at least interested in helping yourself out." He immediately started arranging photos strategically placed on the table.

Now, with his face only a few inches from Dalvin's, he said, "That's right, take a good long look. It's like you've seen a ghost, huh?" His sinister smile released the warmth of his breath, which held remnants of cigarettes, coffee, and more cigarettes.

Dalvin turned away, grimacing.

Mistaking the movement for something other than what it was, both agents jumped at what was assumed - apprehension.

"Okay," chimed Agent Vincent, realizing they weren't making any ground.

"That's perfectly alright; you don't have to say anything. But, if you're not going to help yourself, we'll jut wrap this case up and pin the blame on you."

Dalvin said nothing.

Agent Vincent continued.

"You know, both Scooter and Hasan were CIF's working for us." He paused momentarily, letting his words sink in. Then added, "I guess that date you were so eager to brag about earlier doesn't seem so promising now that you have a murder rap on your head, huh?"

Agent Wallace remained quiet, letting his partner talk. He pulled a cassette recorder from inside his brief case, placing on the table.

Pressing play, they all listened. When Agent Wallace pressed the stop button, there was still silence.

The stillness was finally broken when Agent Vincent reiterated. "When we came in earlier, Dalvin, things got out of hand. I apologize for the both of us. But, I want you to know that we're here to help you, and the only way that can be achieved is if you are willing to help yourself."

Suddenly, Dalvin reflected back to the day of the bike rally on the beach.

Even in his mind, he knew it was fucked up the way Hasan and Scooter went out. But, he also believed in karma. Heaving a long sigh, Dalvin rested his head against the back of his chair. He spoke slowly.

"You know what?" He focused solely on Agent Vincent. "You probably can place me at the beach that day. And yeah, I did speak with Scooter and Hasan, briefly. But, hell, I talked to a lot of other people that day. I got mad numbers from bitches! Did you get that on tape also?"

Both agents fumed. They could care less for Dalvin's arrogance, but at the same time, they needed his testimony.

Knowing he was the critical piece that could link their puzzle together, Agent Vincent tried another approach.

"Look, man," he nearly pleaded, stress mounting in his features. "Helping us possibly could mean the difference of you doing the rest of your life behind some penitentiary wall, or maybe going home in a few months. I know Scooter and Hasan were a far cry from being saints, but, the fact of the matter remains, they were working for the government. Therefore, we can't let their murders just slide under the rug so to speak." Glancing at his partner, he added. "It's true what Scotty says. We'll almost guarantee that you be released in a few months, after we apprehend" he placed a photo in front of Dalvin then finished, "This woman."

Dalvin studied the photo in silence. For some reason, he couldn't remove his thoughts. When first meeting her, he thought she was the most beautiful woman he'd ever seen. She was real. A quality he found attractive and appealing. After learning it was Yasmina the agents were after, Dalvin shrugged his shoulders.

"I don't know that chick. But, if you do find out who she is, let her know that I have a long stretch to do, and I would be obliged if she would consider being my pen pal."

The remark shocked both agents. Agent Vincent, losing his cool, rushed Dalvin, only to be restrained by his partner.

Dalvin continued.

"And another thing," he said, his posture erect in the chair. "As far as them snitch ass niggas, Scooter and Hasan, I don't know who offered them, but I do know this much. If they were working for you... snitching, settin' dudes up, they both got what they deserved."

***

A chuckle escaped Dalvin's mouth at remembering how agitated and angry the two agents were when leaving the prison. It wasn't until that moment when, Kasmir and Shukre, realized the conversation they were having at the table, fell upon deaf ears.

Kasmir spoke first.

"Yo, D., you ai'ight?"

An inquisitive smirk on his face, Dalvin grabbed a white cloth and wiped his mouth.

"Yeah, I'm good. But, I got a little job for you and Shukre that's gon' take some real heart. And it'll definitely help with those high-ass child support payments you got for the next 17 years." Looking in Shukre's direction, he added.

"And you, Mr. 'Bout it 'Bout it, this yo' chance to put everything you've been wolfing about since I came home, to the test."

Although they listened and seemed interested, neither of the two knew what was to come. But they would find out soon enough.

Chapter 7
Toast to the Good Life

Soho is a well-known and costly gated community of Tampa, Florida. Huge 100 year-old birch trees align the streets of million dollar homes with neat manicured cookie-cutter lawns.

With a picturesque view of the Gulf of Mexico in their back yards, the residents of Soho were mayors, judges, doctors, lawyers, and professional athletes. Proud of their stately homes, they regarded this quiet place as utopia, a haven, away from the every day problems that plague society.

One ordinary day, a middle-aged, slightly grayin, gentleman sat on his balcony.

He was doing something he hadn't done in a while. His busy schedule didn't allow it. Out of town on business most days and weeks, the gentleman had finally found a day to relax and enjoy himself. Therefore, he did just that.

As he gazed up at the clear skies, he couldn't help but wonder about the dense and puffy cumulus clouds forming. "Could there be rain in the forecast?" his thoughts questioned. Shunning the thought, he unfastened the beige cardigan robe around his waist, letting it fall to the lawn chair, removed a cigar, an especially imported Padron, from Cuba, out of a black case, ran the leaf the length of his nose, and sighed happily. "Ahhh...the good life!"

Just as he was about to put a flame to the cigar, out walked Maria, the maid.

"Excuse me, Senor...ah, Sir. Jou 'ave a el telefono call. He no mention a nombre."

Quite ruffled by the disturbance, the gentleman groaned, an irritated expression clearly on his face, as he reached for the phone. With a quick wave of the hand, he dismissed Maria like she was a pigeon. Shoo! You can go now."

The cigar crammed between his teeth, the gentleman was once again content.

He had privacy.

"Okay, speak," he uttered, not bothering to ask for a name."

"Well, Mr. L., I mean, Sena...ah, Sir. You won't have to worry about Doc... I mean, he won't be a problem for you anymore," the caller stammered nervously.

Waiting for more information, the gentleman exhaled a cloud of smoke.

"I assume you've gotten what I requested, and are waiting for further instructions?"

The statement was a question directed to the caller. It also held a warning. Realizing this, the caller remained silent, only adding to the gentleman's agitation.

"Well! What is it, Gaietho?" queried the gentleman. "Do you or don't you?"

Gaietho, once a Professional Contract Operative working for the government, was now a hired assassin. He worked for the gentleman. After managing to erase the wrong target, a higher Ranking dignitary of another country, pressure was put on the government to either hand him over, or administer swift punishment, then deliver his head on a platter to them. Either way, they wanted him dead.

Stepping in, the gentleman used his contacts to harbor Gaietho long enough to get him to safety. Now, as he awaited Gaietho's response, he wondered if he had done the right thing by saving him.

"Well…um, yes…I mean, no."

The gentleman abruptly raised from his seated position.

"Goddamn it!" he cursed, adding, "what do you mean, yes…ah..no? The file! The only thing I want is that Goddamned disk. Now, do you have it or not?"

In his anger, he'd managed to crush the cigar into tiny pieces, leaving a tawdry and sour taste in his mouth. Spitting, choking on the strong tobacco, he coughed up what little he could.

"I need that disc. There's too much valuable information encrypted on it. "He mumbled silently as he listened to Gaietho's explanation.

"There was a slight problem, a minor complication." Gaietho said while his accent began to fester in his nervousness. The more he tried explaining, the angrier the gentleman became. In a seething tone, the gentleman said. "You mean to tell me you killed him, and still didn't retrieve the file? He shook his head. "You idiot! Your orders were to commandeer, and if necessary and I reiterated, only if necessary, exterminate, eradicate, and eliminate. Only if you had to."

An opening of silence remained and Gaietho seized the moment.

"Mr. Sena ... I mean, sir. I made sure to cover my tracks. I assur you zat none of zis will lead back to you."

"You Goddamn better not!" he blasted. "The Presidential Election is less than a year away. You damn well better see to it that nothing leads back to my campaign, or my name." His words hung for seconds before continuing, "You do realize you're wanted in Albania for the murder of that Diplomat?"

Gaietho trembled with anger. He knew he had to place the leverage back in his corner. His life depended on it. Not a second after hanging up, he headed for the next clue.

Chapter 8
Precious Temple

Lockdown was over. General population bustled; noisy inmates hustling food throughout the kitchen, rowdy inmates impatiently waiting to exit the stuffy building. Clad in olive-green uniforms, Serosa and Trish joined the ranks of the long single-file line. They entered the hallway.

"Hey, 'youngin!" blared a burly butch female line server. She wore a sweaty bandana tied around her head. "You think you at IHOP or something? This shit ain't gon' get much better than this. Keep it 'movin, or get out the line."

Trish was disturbed. It was hard to manifest the way people at Prag talked.

"And the food," she thought to herself as she ineptly stood, holding the line up. "It looks like slop."

Visually confused, and in a stupor, her thoughts went back to St. Bonaventures, a place where others showed respect, and their meals were tolerable.

Now, at Prag, a place where everything was chaotic, she wondered if she'd be able to cope with the difference of how things were run, and her second test came in the form of the woman who bore the dark eyes. She was creeping slowly on Trish, her weapon at the ready position.

The act was quick and sudden. Before Trish realized what was happening, it was too late.

"I see you waited for me." The baritone voice muttered in Trish's ear, the putrid stench of her breath burned Trish's nostrils.

Scared, frightened, she remained still. She didn't budge. She feared any sudden movement would only add to the pain that was sure to come. Then, something vaguely disturbing dawned on her. "Why haven't I felt pain, yet?"

Since arriving at the facility, Trish already had a heightened sense of something horrible happening to her. And now, that inevitable moment had finally come.

Inmates throughout the chow hall watched in amusement; all wondering when the act would occur. Sherry had other intentions.

Sliding her hand in front of Trish, Sherry's massive forearm tightened around her throat. Her breathing constricted, Trish panicked.

"Shh!" said Sherry, grinding fiercely against the rear of Trish. "Don't make a scene, or it'll get real ugly, fast." Loosening the grip a bit, she uttered, "I'ma make this real sweet for you. You won't feel a thing, that is , unless you decide to fight it."

Realizing the threat for what it truly was, Trish unstubbornly acquiesced.

Sherry's hand slide beneath the fabric of her uniform, fondling Trish's young juvenile nipples. Each time she squeezed, Trish's body tensed; the pain on the brink of excruciating.

Aggressively, Sherry used the hand that once held Trish at bay by the neck, to unfasten the buttons of her trousers. Trish froze, beads of perspiration forming against her clammy skin.

Everyone in the vicinity watched in awe at the taboo unfolding before their very eyes. At each touch, Trish squirmed, fear mounting. She found her voice.

"P..Please," she stammered, tears creasing her eyes. "Don. Don't do this!" was all her mouth could muster when Sherry aggressively slid the length of her middle finger into her vagina.

The pain was abrupt, sharp. Trish, trying as best she could to remain silent, let out a piercing wail that momentarily caused everyone to stop. Silence overcame the busy dining hall. Eyes panned the room in search of the voice. Finding it, some watched in lustful fascination, while others debated on helping. No one made any moves.

For what seem like hours, the interminable display went on. Humiliation, embarrassment, vulgarity, all aided in injuring what little self-respect Trish had left.

Serosa, standing in line at the far side of the dining hall, remained oblivious to what was unfolding, when leaving their cell, she sternly warned Trish to stay near, regardless of what.

Realizing she'd lost sight of Trish when entering the food hall, her eyes hastily roamed the sea of green. Then, she caught movement of Trish.

The atmosphere already held a lot of tension, Serosa figured few wanted to make good on the threats from the day before. Casually walking past others, she strode along the dairy section until she was able to get a better view. What her eyes landed on sent a fierce rage through her, which surprised Serosa with its intensity. .

At one point, she wondered why Trish wasn't fending off Sherry. Then, the memory of an incident between Trish and a staff member of St Bonaventure's resurfaced.

***

The morning had started off as any there. Prayer Service at 7:30 am and class from 10:30 until 2:30 pm.

Trish, the first that morning, entered the confessional. The room was small; adorning a huge marble statue of the Virgin Mary gazing down upon lost souls, theirs.

The second Trish was seated, a view port slid open.

"And who might I ask is wishing to confess their sins today?" mouthed someone. Trish immediately realized it wasn't Father Eckerdsly.

She glanced closer at the port and saw nothing but darkness. A veil-like material hid the face.

In her quest to confess and be forgiven for the horrible crime she had committed that led her to the school, Trish shunned the thought.

Answering, she said, "It's me again, Father. I came by yesterday and was about to tell you about my secret."

The Priest listened.

"I didn't mean to hurt my mother, but, she didn't believe me when I repeatedly told her over and over about what my stepfather was making me do." She wiped her tears, but continued.

"When I refused him, he would punish me by making me do nasty things, things like, touch his..., his thing. Sometimes, he would pinch my chest... You... you know my breasts until they bled."

The entire time she bared her soul, the priest busied himself... listening.

Feeling she was finally coming to a point where the pain of killing her parents was going to be forgiven, Trish was startled by commotion coming from inside the view port.

"My, God Henry! What are you doing? And, why are your pants around your ankles?" it was the voice of Father Eckerdsly.

Feeling betrayed, she burst out of the room in tears.

Finished with her first morning class, Serosa headed down the unusually quiet hallway. Passing up rooms, she stopped at Trish's door. It was open.

"What are you doing sitting on the floor in the dark?"

Trish said nothing.

Seeing there was a bottle of rubbing alcohol situated beside Trish, and what appeared to be tearstains down her cheeks, Serosa bolted down the hallway.

After rushing Trish to the medical ward, days would elapse before Serosa learned that she had tried to commit suicide. Now, as she watched in shock and utter disbelief of what was happening, she remembered why Trish didn't defend herself against Sherry, she couldn't, but it didn't stop Serosa.

Chapter 9
Doubt

After sitting and nervously waiting in the airports' terminal, doubt began to plague Leander.

"I hope she still doesn't harbor resentment over something that happened years ago."

Not particularly talking to anyone, but himself, several times he was inclined to grab his cell phone and call her number, but he waited. Finally, after surfing through the sea of faces making their way over to baggage claim, Leander spotted her.

"Glad to see you guys made it." He ran, giving Benita a hug, kissing Chaunna on the cheek.
It had been years since he'd seen or spoken to his sister.

During childhood, Benita and her younger brother were inseparable. But, betrayal and deceit took its toll, tearing their relationship apart.

The day was beautiful. The May showers, mixing with the sun's rays, made that particular June month one of the prettiest ever. Trees were budding, flowers were blooming and everyone was happy, except Benita.
Her sorority sisters and bride's maids lined the chapel hall dressed in earthly tones.

"But where is Leander, the best man?" an uneasy guest questioned aloud.

Amid the restlessness and murmuring, the pianist played the nuptial song for the third time.

Benita's nervously stood by her hoping and praying their little girl's heart wouldn't be broken.

"Just give him a minute, honey; he's probably experiencing cold feet," her father said helplessly, looking to his wife Mary for help.

The congregation began to murmur loudly regarding the day. Mary felt compelled to ask her husband, "Why don't you go back and see what's taking so long?"

A soft knock at the door went unanswered. Benita's father eyed Mary who indignantly ambled over.

'What's the problem? She asked her voice laced with worry.

No answer.

Both of their faces registered fear that Benita's fiancé had decided not to go forward with the wedding as they simultaneously grabbed the door handle.

An ear-piercing scream followed by Mary spiraling down toward the floor, alerted everyone that something terrible had happened.

Pandemonium engulfed the establishment. People scrambled to see what caused such tragedy.

But, there was in fact, one person who witnessed the travesty, Benita, and now, as she stood facing the one person she despised, she inconceivably fought the urged to choke the life out of him.

"Can you grab our luggage?" she questioned, anything to stave her mind from seeing her brother and her ex-fiancé in that uncompromising position.

Leander jumped at the command. "Sure, sis, anything for you."

Benita gagged.

The S500 Mercedes cruised silently through Nob Hill, an affluent suburb of Portland. Having never been this far west, Benita reeled in the illustrious beauty the city had to offer at night. But in her mind, there was something more dreadful lingering.

"Do you mind stopping so we can get a bite to eat?" She said, without looking in Leander's direction. She looked in the back seat to check on a sleeping Chaunna.

Leander panned his eyes through the rearview mirror, patting Benita's leg. This innuendo didn't fool Benita. She knew his character was tainted, and he wanted badly to be in her grace again, but she wasn't quite ready. She swiftly changed the position of her legs.

"If you guys don't mind," Leander said, feeling the tension, "we're only a few minutes from my place; I'll cook you up a hot meal."

Benita was annoyed by being in his presence; on top of that she was jet-lagged from the long flight. Not up to wrestling with her brother, she lay back against the headrest.

"If you think cooking a hot meal is going to get me to forgive you, you're wrong." She was unaware she actually mumbled the words until Leander asked,

"Huh, what'd you say, sis?"

Turning her head, staring out the window, she averted her attention on the bright twinkling lights in the distance of the Pacific Ocean. A few tankers and naval ships were anchored. Beyond that were the monstrous St. John's Bridge, and the well-lit Rose

Garden Arena where the Portland Trailblazers NBA basketball team played their home games.

The scenery itself was relaxing to the eye. A beauty she hadn't known in a while or at least since Chaunna's illness.

The drive through certain parts of the city reminded Benita of something she didn't see too often. Victorian and Georgian Homes, buildings from the 19th Century still stood, and street car roads connecting different districts. It all held quaintness to it, something different than she was used to, living in Capital Heights.

The car came to a halt at an automated gate. After Leander pushed a few buttons, the gate rose, the car then proceeded to a sub floor parking deck of a condominium.

"Lee, this is nice." Benita observed, not expecting such extravagance.

The comment caused Lee to smile, though his thoughts were elsewhere. He was back at the church, eight years ago, embarrassed that he had been caught with his pants down, destroying his sister's marriage.

It was then he'd vanished off the face of the planet, and if not for the premature death of their parents, he probably would have never heard from Benita again.

The place was huge. For a few seconds, Benita stood in awe. Chandeliers, crystal, two fire places, an elevator. "An elevator!" she mouthed incredulously.

Chapter 10
Trouble

The late model Ford careened, almost tipping on its side as it sped dangerously around the corner. If not for the crossing guard directing the rambunctious teens who impatiently waited for traffic to clear, the scene would have been gruesome.

Gaietho, banging viciously against the dashboard, cursed. "Fuck! This isn't how I planned it." He sped recklessly down the interstate.

The original plan consisted of accosting Brittany from her home. That plan went out the window when Gaietho realized the trouble it would take. The neighbors. Going to plan B, he discreetly followed Cary in her BMW SUV, and watched as Brittany climbed out and made her way in the schools building.

2:45 p.m. rolled around. Just as the other vehicles filed in along the curbside, Gaietho anonymously sidled, blending in-- or so he thought.

The guard worked at the private school for the last three years. As soon as the rust-colored Ford parked against the curb, his radar went up.

Instinctively, he began walking in the direction of the strange truck. Over the years, he'd become acquainted with the families whose kids went to the private school, but "This vehicle," he muttered to himself, "is out of place. Let me introduce myself, maybe another student's parents are in the vehicle."

Gaietho was aware of the man's approach. With caution, he watched the guard, his hand easing to the gun situated in the passenger's seat. The man moved closer, a smile creased at the corner of his mouth, his hand nearing the holstered gun at his side. He peered at the dark tint, nothing. Slowing his approach, he unfastened the clasp around his weapon after hearing the car's engine idle.

Gaietho peered into the rearview mirror. Another man approaching, but he was a guard. He too was unfastening his weapon.

Nervously, Gaietho began to sweat. "This is not what I'm paid to do." He mouthed through clenched teeth. "I'm a professional killer, not a kidnapper."

As the words left his mouth, an image of his mother, and her last words to him resurfaced.

"…Gaietho! Run…run for your life. Don't let these people turn you into what they are."

Gaietho was now sweating profusely as his dark curly hair matted against his forehead. Shaking his head, trying to rid himself of the memory, the scene continued to unfold.

"…you Satan, how do you call yourself a Muslim, a child of Allah, when you run around kidnapping and murdering innocent people?"

His mother was covered from head to toe in all white. Only her eyes and hands were visible. She was deeply rooted in her religion and tried to rear Gaietho in the true Muslim religious teachings.

But this day, as the two men who vowed to steal young Gaietho away and train him to become an

Islamic extremist, who will one day become a foot soldier in the war against the west, she vowed to not let it happen.

Gaietho was young, no more than eight. He didn't understand why his own people killed young and old men alike for not participating in their "cause," and his mother's pleading cry still rang in his head.

"Please, let me have my son. I will raise him to be a proper Muslim, not some murderer's belief."

For seconds, Gaietho was tugged at; pulled this way by his mother, jerked that way by the two men. To his surprise, he watched as his mother raised a sharp knife over his head.

"I'll kill him before I let you destroy him." With that, she fixed her mouth to say, "All praises due to Al…"

The force of the AK-47 ripped through her body. Blood splattered over Gaietho as he stood in shock, watching his mother's tiny body collapse to the floor, her white garments drenched in red.

Engulfed by the memory that had just played through his mind, he was brought back to present when a tap at his driver's side tinted window broke his dream state.

The vehicle violently jerked away from the corner. Everyone watching screamed in panic as the guard approaching from the front went sailing ten feet into the air. His body landed with a thud. Dead on impact.

In the moments following, Gaietho realized the new depth of his situation. Police would be scouring, combing every inch of the city for his vehicle. T.V.

stations from all across the country would air the incident. A lengthy attempt at finding who was the cause of it would ensue, but the one thing that troubled him more than any of this, was explaining to his employer why and how this unfortunate accident happened.

Chapter 11
Surviving at all Cost

Serosa stared in disbelief as memories of being inappropriately touched by Henry flashed through her mind. This caused her rage to increase. Now, only a few feet behind Sherry, who insistently, with no care in the world, whispered insult after insult in Trish's ear, she prepared herself.

"Let her go!"

Sherry, who was engrossed in fondling Trish with more than one finger, heard the comment, but shrugged it off. The cries and pleas coming from Trish elevated her greed, causing her to wrap her legs, entwining Trish like two snakes mating.

Again, Serosa mouthed, "Let her go!" this time, grabbing Sherry's shoulder and squeezing.

Sherry immediately fell to her knees. "Aauuugh!" she screamed from the pain that shot through her body.

The crowd was silent. Not one person spoke.

Serosa, now standing directly over Sherry, added more pressure.

"Bitch, I told you to let her go the first time." She cursed, raised her knee, and brought it down hard, in the dead center of Sherry's spine. Another yelp escaped her mouth.

The crowd gathered closer. Everyone was fighting to get a better look, clambering to view Sherry in distress.

Serosa shocked herself with the abrupt anger. For seconds her memory flashed on the roommate she'd murdered. This frightened her.

Ever since that day, she'd fought savagely to suppress her rage, fearing that she'd one day do it again. Now, as she peered into Sherry's eyes with venomous hatred, she wondered where this new rage came from.

At the time, back when Serosa underwent the horrific bouts of torture at St. Bonaventrues, she could vaguely recall an instance when she'd overheard something that shook her to the core. "Here," said the gentleman, the Senator, who remained behind Dr. Carmichael as he examined Serosa. He handed the doctor a small vile.

"What's this?" Dr. Carmichael asked a bewildered expression across his face.

Gently lifting a syringe from the doctor's pocket, he said, "Do you mind?"

Serosa, watching this, squirmed. Her eyes pleaded for help from a person she knew couldn't help her.

The small pinpoint of the needle disappeared as it burrowed deep into her arm. Looking back at Dr. Carmichael, the Senator said, "It's one of my latest inventions, a new and innovative drug that's going to change the world of technological medicine, and corner the market. This is my friend." He held the vile aloft, "Meet…Cehyazyli…"

Not remembering much about that day, Serosa shivered at the thought of the serum injected into her, and realized when she was in danger, the effects the medicine seemed to manifest. But trying to make sense of her situation cost her.

In one deft move, Sherry swept her arm forward. It wasn't until Serosa felt the burning sensation she realized she'd been cut.

"Yeah, Bitch!" Sherry cursed, smiling. She was on her feet. "You thought this was a game? Come in here and disrupt something that has nothing to do with you."

Serosa said nothing. She stood holding her side, blood seeping between her fingers.

The crowd was now hyped again. Whistling rowdy chants of "Serosa, Serosa" that echoed through the dining hall.

A hand fished deep into her trousers, Serosa withdrew a blade she'd stashed in her waistline. Circling each other, both women awaited the right moment to make a move.

The place was in frenzy. Food trays clapped against tabletops. Cups banged. Roaring threats and insults assaulted anyone who would listen. Now, the circle which encamped the two women grew smaller.

Serosa didn't realize the gravity of the situation. Well aware that walking away wasn't an option, she was unaware of how tight the circle had become. But as she stumbled, not realizing Trish was close behind her, the foot to her ribcage caused her to lose all of her air, that's when reality set in.

"Get up, bitch!" Sherry kicked her a second time.

Still clutching at her side, Serosa fought for air. Everything around her was quickly closing and claustrophobia was setting in.

Desperation even began to reel itself when she threw a wild kick at sherry. This caused her blade to slide from her hand and as she frantically searched between an on looker's feet, it was apparent that she would never find it.

She was about to surrender; taking whatever beating she had to from Sherry, when out the corner of her eye, she saw something shiny. The blade was buried beneath Trish's foot.

With a huge thrust, Sherry's arm snaked, her blade racing for the side of Serosa's neck. But a surprise blow to the gut stunned her. Serosa connected. Dropping her blade, Sherry then scrambled to the floor in search of her weapon.

Just as she had done, Serosa did the same.

"How does it feel, bitch!" she kicked Sherry hard in the ribcage.

Again, everyone went wild, and for a second, Serosa found herself enjoying this.

But, the time had come for her to make a decision. She knew she couldn't let Sherry live.

One last kick sent a dazed Sherry sailing to the floor. With a knee placed on her gut, Serosa brought the blade to Sherry's throat.

"Bitch!" if you had only listened. "She said, as the sharp serrated edge of the blade dug into Sherry's skin.

The crowd still chanted, "Kill her, kill her!"

Serosa knew that killing Sherry was easy. She also realized that she had less than twelve months left, and she would be free. Free to go home, free to return to her family. Then it dawned on her. "What do I have left? I have no family, friends, nothing. Maybe this is where God wants me to be."

While in her troubled thoughts, she was unaware of the crowd parting. They weren't chanting anymore, either. Her hand gripping the razor, Serosa desperately fought the urge to kill this woman she didn't know. But, something was forcing her. And it wasn't until she heard Sherry mouthed, "Who's going to fight her battles when you're gone, huh?" and she realized Sherry was right.

Despite the question posed and the ones she struggled with in her own mind, Serosa realized the matter at hand is what was important. Getting within an inch of Sherry's ear, she said, "You know, you may be right. I can't protect her forever, but as long as I'm here, I'll be damned if I let you take advantage of her, Bitch!"

Her arm viciously swung forward, the blade moving in the direction of Sherry's heart. However, before the force could penetrate Sherry's chest cavity, a strong hand seized Serosa's wrist.

Every inmate watching this unfold stood in shock, unable to fathom who, and why this person would interfere. They soon found out.

"Deena! Deena!" Lottie called a second time. "She's not worth it."

Looking over her shoulder, Serosa gave a puzzled stare at the woman peeling the blade from her hand. "What?" was all she could utter.

Grabbing Serosa and Trish by the arm Lottie gestured at the entrance of the dining hall. "Come on, you gotta get out of here."

Seconds later, the dining hall swarmed with armed CO's demanding everyone hit the floor, or suffer the consequences. It was at this time when Serosa looked to the sky mouthing a silent thanks to Benita.

Chapter 12
Danger Lurking

The gale winds shifting past the Volvo were drowned out by deep thoughts, admirable ones, Henry felt for his friend, mentor and co-worker, Dr. Carmichael.

He left the gala early; a ceremony held in the memory of the doctor and his heart was heavy. The memory of that dyspeptic morning, the one in which his friend was murdered, plagued him. "I had no idea someone was threatening his life," he pondered.

As Henry breathed the words, he remained somber, somewhat reserved, drumming his fingers against the steering wheel.

"The disc." He wondered, thinking back to the file he'd hidden. "What was so important on it that someone would kill him?"

Still not finding the answer, Henry squinted his eyes against the bright headlights of oncoming vehicles. "I erased everything on it. The entire file."

His melancholy mood definitely needed lifting. Leaning in, about to press the button to turn on the satellite radio station, Henry became aware of a sound, a chime emitting from his console.

Glancing at the computerized system, the words, INCOMING CALL was illuminated, followed by UNIDENTIFIED NUMBER. He pressed a button.

"Yes!"

The moment the voice sounded in his ear, Henry froze, his heart skipping a beat. His pulse racing, he began to sweat profusely. He pulled off onto the median.

Henry nervously squirmed in his seat, biting his lip, the engine idling as his foot trembled against the break pad, in a state of shock and disbelief; he couldn't believe what he was hearing. Then, a notion came to him

Ever since the mysterious death of his mentor, there had been moments when both he and Carey sensed that something was not quite right. They had a feeling of being watched. Henry's mind replayed the clip from the news when the crossing guard was run down in front of Brittany's school.

"Could the two be related?" Henry shook the thought, thinking of an earlier conversation held at the dinner table that evening

"I agree," Cary voiced, "we're probably overreacting from paranoia. After all, this is D.C., and I'm quite sure that not only are blacks committing crimes, so are the Lobbyists, Politicians and hell, even the President of the United States is robbing us blind - corruption is everywhere."

As for the thought of securing a safe environment, while giving his family a taste of the good life, Henry realized that no one in America, his country, was safe.

Lafayette Square nestled in the center of a very picturesque downtown Washington D.C. It was minutes away from the White House, cafés, bistros and restaurants of all kinds. The area was extremely diverse, had the best nightclubs, museums, and newly refurbished hotels; these factors were part of the culture in which he now resided.

"How could this have happened?" he questioned himself in silence.

After blowing the mission in front of the private school, Gaietho went back to his original plan.

Bright and early one morning, creeping in with the fog that rolled in, Gaietho made his move.

He knew in order to achieve the objective, he would have to either, kill one and take the other, or abduct them both. He chose the latter.

Henry felt he was being punished for all of his profane acts and wrongdoings. With what little composure he could muster, he stammered, "Wh...What is it that you want? Where are my wife and daughter?"

Gaietho laughed in his ears. There was no empathy.

"What I want, Henry is for you to bring me the disc."

Henry swallowed a throaty gulp.

"Could this be the same person who killed Dr. Carmichael?" he questioned, not aware that he thought aloud.

"Zat's right, Henry, I am the person responsible." Fear gripped Henry as the man continued. "It may be in your best interest to find what I want and co..."

"Where are my wife and daughter?" Henry interrupted, anger and fear consuming him. Continuing he added, "You son of a bitch. There had better not be one single hair harmed on them."

Gaietho interrupts this time.

"Now, now Henry," he said his voice calm. "Zat's no way to treat a person, someone as crazy as I am." Pausing, he added, "I killed the doctor, and the crossing guard who was a little bit too curious about my vehicle being parked in front of your daughter's school, and I won't hesitate to kill these two beautiful women before me."

Panic set in as Henry said, "Okay, look! I…I 'm sorry for the outburst, but please, I'll do whatever you want. Just don't hurt my family."

The only thing Henry knew about this man was, he held a distinct accent, one of a foreign country; Middle East. And, he was a sociopath. Realizing how unstable this person may be, he decided to go along, until he had time to alert the authorities.

But, before the thought could fester, Gaietho said, "Don't worry, Henry, your family will be alright. As long as you deliver, no harm will come to them. And Henry," he said, the grogginess to his accent giving no hint of emotion, "It's also in your best interest to not involve the authorities. If I smell or think that you are deceiving my orders, you'll never see your family again. Are we clear?"

Henry found himself shaking his head. "Yes, we're clear."

Chapter 13 -
A Bond or...

Benita enjoyed the moist pacific air. She also couldn't shake the fact of Oregon's amorous beauty. The place was out of this world. However, there was reality that she'd been at Leander's home for six days, and he hadn't done as much as hinted at helping with Chaunna's hospital costs.

"Lee, I want you to know that we've really enjoyed ourselves."

A big smile crossed his lips. He felt delighted to know that she once again approved of him.

For the longest, he knew his sister resented him, hated his guts. But, the entire week together, he felt a bond that reminded him of the one they'd shared when they were kids. Embracing Benita in a hug, he said, "Sis, I can't lie, I missed you so much over the years. I mean, there was a void inside of me... something missing that only a sibling could fill, and I want you to know that I enjoyed your company, as well as Chaunna's too.

I know what happened at your wed..." Benita immediately placed a hand in his face.

"Look, I don't want to re-visit that day. Let's not talk about that."

Truth of the matter was she couldn't believe he would bring up such a disgusting topic. She moved to a chaise lounge that sat on the balcony. The view overlooked most of the city.

Not bothering to look back at her brother, Benita said, "Lee, we've been here for six days now. Our tickets cost over $2,000 dollars. And I know I probably should've used that money towards the hospital costs, but I needed a break." After a brief pause, she continued. "Why haven't you even offered to help me with Chaunna's medical costs? You know you're all I have left."

Lee had already felt the stirrings of what Benita's real reason for making the trip, money. But, he wanted to be sure. Then, as he moved to stand beside her, he noticed an amorphous gaze in her eyes. But it wasn't tears. It was a look, a far-away gaze, one of a person stricken to deal with an almost certain loss.

He extended a hand, resting it on her shoulder.

"Sis, you know if there's anything you need, anything, I'm here for you."

The gentleness of his tone, the sincerity in which his words came, eased Benita's mind. "Thank you, God!" she mouthed in silence. For a moment, she thought she would have to foot this journey alone.

At that exact moment, a bond was shared. Each faced losing someone they loved dearly before this abrupt visit, but now, there seemed to be a chance, a chance for life and a chance of rekindling a relationship. Handing over an envelope, Benita embellished, "I'm gonna need you in a big way."

Silence remained as Leander perused the contents of the envelope. A tenebrous expression shadowed his face, telling a story of sorrow.

"Lymphoblast Leukemia," he whispered in disbelief. Lee had heard of the disease before, but not in his wildest imagination did he ever think someone in his family would be stricken with the life-threatening disease.

"She's only 16, he mouthed again. "My goodness! Why now, God?"

Though he was speaking to himself, Lee was unaware of Benita hearing his reaction to the news. And, in his eyes, he couldn't fathom how well she was taking all of this. His emotions flared. Moving to the balcony's edge, his posture wavered, shoulders slumped. He continued reading.

"Chaunna's gotta have a Bone Marrow Transplant!" he voiced incredulously, without glancing down at his sister.

The moment the words left his mouth, tears gushed from Benita's eyes. For the first time since hearing the dreadful news from doctors, she allowed herself to mourn. She cried uncontrollably.

It wasn't the fact of the type of disease that bothered Benita. Hearing the dread in the voice of others is what ached her. She knew how long a bone marrow transplant recipient had to wait. Some never got the chance to receive the surgery.

They died.

As hard as she tried to be strong, the rock that Chaunna needed at a time such as this, she knew the only person who could change things was God.

Blotting at tears that managed to slide the length of his cheeks, Leander knelt beside Benita.

"It's gonna be okay, sis. I'll make sure of that."

Although she felt defeated and her emotions unraveled, Benita felt there was hope. And when, Leander asked, "How much money do you need?" The ray of hope blossomed into a beautiful rainbow on a cloudy day. It was the best she'd felt in a while. She finally had someone by her side.

Chapter 14
Bamboozled

"And this, I promise you!" said the Senator.

The elections were in full swing. He boldly stood behind the podium, gloating, boasting about the changes he planned to make within the government. "If elected as President," he voiced to the many in attendance, "I will devote my life to putting a stop on terrorism, changing health care reform, revising our foreign policy, and seeing to it that, not only the large corporations are penalized for misappropriating funds, but I intend to do that same thing, right here, in Congress."

Before he was able to utter another word, a voice shouted, "How do you intend on doing that when it's people like yourself controlling everything that goes on in these places? There's nothing but corrupt officials!" He finished.

The validity of the question ruffled the senator.

Being a Senator for as long as he had been, he knew that every politician's goal was to achieve a certain status of power. Very seldom did one come with positive and legal views that would aid society as a whole. And the ones who put greed over the welfare of people first, spin the truth, twisted the truth, and distributed unadulterated prevarications to deceive the people about what their real intentions are. They lied to the public.

Now, as every eye filtering throughout the crowd focused on the gentleman posing the questions, the Senator answered.

"Well sir, I can assure you that over the years, we've seen, and even have been subjected to the wrongs of many of our leaders. But, you can't let one rotten apple stop you from making apple pie," he smiled, arousing a cheer from the crowd. He suddenly turned serious.

"Now, as I was stating before the interruption, if elected as your President, I can assure you all that any and all corruption, on my watch, will not be tolerated. It doesn't matter what level, or position they may hold. Swift justice will be served."

The crowd clapped, applauding the answer given by the Senator. However, unbeknownst, a lone gentleman, shielded by a hat, stood out of eyesight of the attendees, resolutely eyeing the vociferous heckler.

The crowd was enlivened; yelling, screaming, waiving banners around, and hoisting posters at the sight of their new and prospective President. Leaning his entire six foot-one-inch frame over the podium, the senator reverently waved and smiled at the excited crowd as he delivered his final message.

"People, I vow to uphold the laws of our solemn nation. Crime will not be tolerated in this country, and breaking laws in other countries abroad will not go unpunished. Every citizen will be able to ride public transportation and feel safe. And lastly," he raised a finger, scanning the faces of the attendees. "Every citizen will know that they are safe inside their own homes. This my people, is what I, Edgar

L'Enfants III, promise you, if and when I'm elected as your next President of the United States of America. Thank you."

Despite the humidity in the air, the crowd remained hopeful. It would become everyone's chance at having a stable economic future. No more mortgage crisis or homes being foreclosed. No more sky rocketing fuel prices. And no more spending tax dollars bailing big corporations out of their financial ruts. They all remained hopeful, knowing that this man, Senator Edgar L'Enfants, could be the one to give them this dream.

The Senator recognized the glimmer in their eyes. "I've got them!" he thought as he waved and smiled. "If they only knew my real objective."

The state of Florida's track record for voting corruption was the worst in history. The last few Presidents and Governors, honed an impenetrable network with public officials, thus resulting in unanimous wins for Republicans. and today wouldn't be any different.

With elections wrapping up, Senator L'Enfants felt at ease. Although a slim margin of points remained between him and the other candidate, he was confident he'd win the state. "Amnesty is powerful!" he mouthed, walking off the stage. He made it aboard his campaign bus.

The phone rang.

"Senator L'Enfants speaking."

He was on the way to his stateroom when the voice stunned him. He stopped. Walking forward, peering through the window, he assured the coast was clear before saying, "How did you come by this number?" he asked defensively. "Never mind that," he added, loosening his tie-flinging it to the chair. "I take it you have something for me this time."

Silence.

Gaietho pondered on whether he should inform the Senator on the latest events. The hit and run. He waited a little too long.

"Well!" the Senator blasted, clearly agitated.

"No...Sir, I haven't retrieved Zee document yet. But, I'd..."

The tie was now in the Senator's hand, being wrung around is knuckles. Imprints remained as blood became constricted.

"Damn it! I've told you more than once that I can't afford any other mistakes, or accidents, as you so lightly put them. First, it was the doctor you killed, then God knows whatever else you neglected to tell me. And, you still don't have the disc." He paused momentarily. "I simply asked you to take care of something and you somehow managed to screw it up."

It was now or never for Gaietho to reveal his new discovery.

"Sir," he said hesitantly. "I'm very close to finding the disc. I don't want to disclose over the phone what I have, but I assure you, it won't be much longer."

Shaking his head unbelievingly, the Senator said, "I'm sure you're right, Gaietho. Just like when you killed the crossing guard, I guess he played a significant part in locating the files, huh?"

Senator L'Enfants, after hanging up, exhaled a huge sigh. "Not one person I ask to do something gets it right the first time around." His thoughts went to a different time, a time when he faced betrayal within his own ranks. He was bamboozled.

***

"Adam," Senator L'Enfants called from the small walkie-talkie he held in his hand. "I need you to come around to the balcony." He was upset by the call he'd received from Gaietho. The one where he murdered the doctor, but didn't retrieve the disc.

Stepping from beneath an awning just below the deck, Adam looked up and said, "I'm right here, Senator." This shocked him.

Adam Tinkerton had been working with the Senator for the past eight years. Superfluously, he exceeded what his original job title called for, running errands.

Yet, year after year of having been promised that another higher position would be allotted to him, Tinkerton quickly realize that he would be an assistant forever if he didn't take matters in his own hands.

Greenhaven Center sat on seven acres of Tampa's most vegetated green in the city. Membership for the golf resort reared from politicians, many like the Senator himself, judges, corporate lawyers, doctors, all, who in a sense, held vestige amounts of power, or the connections to someone.

Aiding as caddy that day, another benefit of his job as an assistant, Tinkerton stood aside while the senator browsed the expansive green.

"Sir, what size iron will you be using today?" he asked.

Senator L'Enfants was dressed in a pair of beige slacks, a black Izod shirt, and a large Jack Nichols hat. A huge Padron cigar crammed between his lips; he turned, pointed and said, "I think I'll use that 13 iron. See if I can drive that baby down the lane."

The entire course was empty, save for a few others who were centered around the fifth hole. Positioning himself, legs apart, hands tightly gripping the club, the Senator heaved a powerful swing, sending the ball sailing hundreds of yards in the air.

He watched, using his hands as a shield from the sun. Tinkerton, on the other hand, stared at the Senator, wondering if he should say anything,

"Hey! Wadaya think!" exclaimed the senator as he startled Tinkerton. "That baby went what... hundred fifty or two hundred yards?"

The remark came as a surprise, catching Tinkerton off guard. He was busy convincing himself that what he was about to attempt was warranted. The senator noticed his discourse.

"Is everything alright, Adam? You look like your mind's a thousand miles away."

Senator L'Enfants was about to inquire about his family when Tinkerton said, "Well sir, there's something important that needs to be discussed, and I have to be frank with you. It's not going to be pleasing to the ears."

Placing the golf club back inside the bag, the Senator slid his leather gloves off. He stood tall, hands akimbo on his hips and his gaze was one of concern.

"Is it Susan?" He inquired, referring to Tinkerton's wife. "The marriage… is it in trouble?"

Shaking his head, Tinkerton said, "No, it's nothing like that." His demeanor spoke volumes.

Before the senator could utter another word, Tinkerton fired away.

"Look, sir there's no easy way to say this so I'll be blunt. I know about the trouble you're in."

The look Senator L'Enfants gave Tinkerton bore holes into him. For moments, no golf clubs sounded - smacking against balls, motors of golf carts humming, nothing. He just stared unblinkingly at Tinkerton.

Anger lines underlying the few wrinkles on his face, the Senator blared,

"What do you mean…trouble I'm in?" And what is it you think you know?"

Tinkerton's heart raced. His career was over. "How am I going to explain to Susan that I got fired for an accusation I thought to be something else?"

Working for the Senator for so many years, there were many times he'd stumbled upon scams that his boss, the Senator, and other colleagues, committed. He turned a blind eye. And like the loyal subordinate he was, he never mentioned anything to anyone, about the benchmarks his employer received for his own self-interest projects. The government funds he misappropriated, tax breaks from interior decorators, kick backs from large corporations. Never, ever had he mentioned this, nor did his employer offer him any of it.

Now, standing before the man he once admired, it angered him that throughout his eight years of service, he wasn't given a raise, acknowledged for the work he'd done, or received a mere 'thank you.' In so few words, he knew he wouldn't be climbing that ladder of success anytime soon, unless he resulted to drastic means of securing a position.

Looking the Senator directly in his eyes, Tinkerton said, "If you have to ask, it's not what I think I may know. It's what I definitely know." He produced a tape recorder, pressing the play button.

It didn't take long for the Senator to realize the situation he faced.

"Alright!" he irritably stated. "What is it you want?"

Tinkerton said nothing.

"Damn it!" the Senator cursed, clearly angered that he was cornered. "Tell me something. I'm quite sure we can come to some sort of agreement. Whadaya say I give you a raise?"

Tinkerton showed no emotion.

"Okay then," said the Senator. "What about a change in your job description?" He caught what he thought to be a glimmer from Tinkerton. "Well, then that's it. First thing tomorrow, I'll move you up another level to Campaign Manager."

Tinkerton shook his head.

"What then?" The Senator asked, not clear on what the man wanted.

When Tinkerton finally spoke, the Senator spat out the crushed remnants to the cigar almost choking on himself. For seconds, he remained crouched, holding his chest, his face bloodshot red.

Merely twenty feet away were two men approaching. As they neared, one said, "My God, Edgar, are you alright?" It was his neighbor, Carl Weiss, a Circuit Court Judge.

Raising a hand, the Senator shook his head assuring the men he was okay, adding, "I'm perfectly okay, a little too much sun maybe." Eyeing Tinkerton, he said, "I think I'll have my Vice...I mean, my assistant take me back home. I need some rest."

Tinkerton gloated inside. He knew he had him. Grabbing the Senator's arm, he said, "Come, sir, lets get you out of this heat." He smiled at the men.

"Get your damn hands off me!" replied the Senator, jerking away.

Chapter 15
Smoke Screen

Despite the contentious altercation between Serosa and Sherry, the latter part of the day seemingly went without incident. Inmate after inmate filed out to the recreation yard.

Situated in a corner, away from the hustle and bustle of inmates exercising, some on the pull-up bars, others walking the track, and a few engaged in a fierce game of handball, sat Serosa, Trish and Lottie. They were engulfed in a conversation about the way things worked at Prag - unaware of the eyes watching them.

"'Whadaya wanna bet that by the end of the night, she'll have both them bitches eating her pussy?" a heavy set female said, referring to Lottie.

"Shit!" quipped another female. "We all know the answer to that one. Question is, what about Sherry? I mean, that bitch won't even fuck with Lottie, that bitch is crazy!"

Everyone went silent at the mention of Lottie. As for the two females gathered together, they clearly recall the rumors they had heard about her, and wanted no part of anything, when it came to her.

Excitedly, Serosa and Trish watched in silence as two women went back forth. The rubber ball was smacking against the wall with tremendous force. Aggressively, they battled. Sweat dripping from each one.

Amused by the competitive nature of the women, Serosa wondered, "Why can't everyone get along like that?" Before she could continue her thoughts, she was interrupted when Lottie said, "There's a lot you two are going to have to 'learn if you're 'goin to survive in herre." She noticed the contemptuous looks in their eyes.

Discreetly, without much movement, Lottie shifted her position.

Pointing, she added, "You see those two?" referring to the Mexican women battling on the handball court. "They walked onto that court as friends." Pausing, she looked for the confused expressions she knew would surface on the faces of Serosa and Trish. Continuing, she added, "Before that game is over, they will be enemies, if they don't kill each other."

She then smiled as the bewildered expression came to Serosa's face, first.

"I don't get it!" Serosa admonished. "Why would they fight, or become enemies?" It's just a game of handball."

Lottie laughed. Instinctively, she moved closer, brushing the back of her hand against Serosa's face. Memories of the times they'd shared in the past began to surface. However, it was one memory that seemed to fester that wouldn't go away, and no matter how hard she tried, she couldn't shake it.

***

The flight was 12 hours long. When her feet finally touched American soil, Lottie smiled.

An airline flight attendant, she'd just arrived back at Patrick Henry International Airport in Newport News, Virginia, the flight arriving from England. Having been in a sound relationship the past five years, the only thing she wanted to do was slide into the warmth of a hot bubble bath, sip a cool glass of Chardonnay, and relax in the soothing arms of her lover. Unfortunately, things wouldn't turn out as she'd planned.

After having climbed three flights of stairs, Lottie stood just outside of her door, tired. Her breathing was labored and her feet ached.

A tap sounded at the door almost seconds after she removed the four-inch heels from her feet.

Nothing.

She wondered why Deena would have the music blasting so loud when there was a no noise policy in her rental agreement. Slightly disturbed, and angered by the thought, she fished through her shoulder bag, coming up with the keys. She inserted them in the doorknob.

Deena and her friends were unaware of the intruder. They were oblivious to anything or anyone as they indulged in acts of sex on the living room floor; flying high by the X they'd taken earlier.

Lottie was shocked. Stunned. Stymied.

Standing with her mouth opened, she couldn't find the words to say. Her heart wrenched, achingly terribly, she was genuinely affected by what was unfolding before her very eyes.

She tried swallowing. Her throat dry and perched wouldn't let her. For seconds, she stood on weak and trembling legs, using the doorway as an upright to balance on. She was in a state of disbelief as she thought of everything she had done for Deena.

However, her hurtful questions were overshadowed by the intense moaning perforating her eardrums.

She rested against the door and wall, still trying to reconcile in her mind that what was happening, really wasn't. Her heart told her a different story.

Lottie's arteries thumped. Her breathing came in shallow bouts. Rage consumed her, knowing the prospect of something violent might happen, was out of her control.

She would have preferred walking away, rethinking the situation, but she couldn't

Witnessing the penetration of the man's penis, inexorably sliding in and out, causing Deena to cry out in demonic pleasure, shattered all hopes of rationale. Lottie was wounded. A deer caught in the blinding crossfire of head lights from an approaching vehicle, then, their eyes met for the first time.

Deena was on her third orgasm. The numbing effect of the X, and the painful pleasure of sex had her in another world. It was then that the others realized someone else was in the equation.

Lottie's presence, that portentous look of evil in her eyes staring unblinkingly, warned of her distress. Slowly, they tried to part. Their foreboding looks mimicked a child who'd done wrong. But, it wasn't until Lottie's sister, Janae came strolling out of the bathroom, in the nude, when all sense of reality was abandoned.

An hour passed before police and forensics crime scene specialists arrived. And as described by a lead detective, a 21-year veteran of the force, the crime was as horrendous as any he'd ever seen.

On the kitchen table lay a butcher's knife, dry blood congealing over it's metal blade. Blood splotches decorated the white walls. But the most grotesque of all was seeing Deena's male lover with half his severed penis still engorged inside her vagina, both of their throats slit from ear to ear. This left Janae.

When arriving on the scene, police thought it to be odd that they'd find someone alive. But there she was, crammed into a corner, a catatonic heap. The brutal slaughter pushed her into a psychiatric coma.

Lottie's thoughts were interrupted as Serosa said, "Look, I don't know what it is with you people in here trying to take advantage of others, rubbing our hands, faces and whatnot." She eyed Lottie seriously, and then added, but, I'm not with that shit. And for that matter, no one's going to take advantage of her," she referred to Trish. "While I'm at this place."

Things were quiet for seconds before Serosa added, "I don't know the reason you're here, much less know your name, but if a friend is what you're looking for, I will be that. Nothing more." Lottie sheepishly turned away. Something caught her attention.

Realizing this, Serosa asked, "And, why do you keep calling me Deena?"

Serosa's questioned went unanswered when someone yelled, "You cheated, bitch!" It was the surly black woman, playing handball, she was pointing her racket at the other woman.

Aware of what was about to ensue, Lottie grabbed both Serosa and Trish by the arm and said, "We need to get out of here."

They were too late.

The velocity of the racket being swung sounded. The impact in which it connected was even louder. The Mexican woman fell to the ground. Blood leaked freely from an open gash in her skull.

"Come on!" Lottie yelled. She was in a trotting gait. "We need to get off this yard."

From out of nowhere came hoards of inmates, blacks and Mexicans. With stones, shanks, metal, wood, whatever could be used as a weapon. They angrily pummeled any hue that wasn't their own. A riot had ensued.

Sirens blared, riot police geared up. They came in droves of twelve, fifteen, and thirty. Soon after, percussion grenades exploded. The crackling sounds of automatic weapons fired. It was everyone's last and final warning. "Hit the ground or become a permanent fixture."

Over the next few days, the entire compound remained on lockdown. It would also be when Serosa faced danger she didn't realize was waiting for her around the corner.

Chapter 16
Ante Up

"Yo, D," Kasmir quipped as he eyed the equipment. "You wasn't bull-shitting when you said you had a job for us. Who we hittin, the 'mutha-fuckin President of the United States or something?"

Browsing through the vast array of merchandise scattered across the floor; AR-15's, 50 Caliber Desert Eagles, M-1 Assault rifles, AK-47's, Grenades, and Grenade launchers, Kasmir couldn't believe his eyes.

The weaponry sat atop various crates labeled, PROPERTY OF THE US GOVERNMENT. Under Article 3 Section 2178, anyone caught in possession of stolen merchandise from the U.S.Military, are subject to federal prosecution. The penalties range from life imprisonment and fines up to one million dollars under statute 001N7F1G of the Uniform Code of Military Justice.

Shukre was too busy wielding the barrel of an AR-15 around to notice the affixed label.

Weeks ago, after receiving the call from Damita, Dalvin didn't know what to make of the conversation. She wasn't precise, only divulging that he should meet her at a neutral place.

It was the month of October and the weather was moderately sunny. As for Damita, Portland's climate was rainy and cool, but she couldn't deny the fact of the tepid air flowing in from Myrtle Beach's coast, felt good on her skin.

Damita and Dalvin slowly strolled along the shore as huge waves cascaded at their feet. The mild sand felt good as it sifted through their toes.

"Being back here feels sort of weird, huh?" Damita asked. She'd stopped walking, feeling they were out of earshot of the few other hand-holding couples that strolled slowly by, lost in their own worlds.

Dalvin faced her. " I know whatchu' mean, cuz. She is sort of spooky." He laughed and pointed at a sky that was turning murky red.

Darkness was on its way, and the sun mixing with the clouds painted an eerie picture across the horizon.

An unspoken silence remained.

From where they stood, chains of hotels could be seen aligning the beachfront. And subliminally, their thoughts paralleled, briefly taking them back to that day.

Damita broke the silence.

"Look, we can reminisce some other time. Right now, we need to discuss some business."

Dalvin displayed no emotion. For a second, he thought she was referring to the drug game, until she added. "I know you're probably thinking drugs, but that's not why I brought you out here."

Dressed in a pair of grey Mob sweats and a wife beater, Dalvin's mind involuntarily went back to that fateful day at the bike rally, and then to the day he was interrogated in prison. He shrugged off the thought.

"Cuz," he said eyeing Damita. "You know I'm down for whatever. I mean shit, you held me down when I came home. Two million dollars, who would've expected something that gangsta? How can I say no?" he paused before adding,

"If it weren't for you, I'd either be dead trying to make a lick, or facing life throwing bricks at the penitentiary. But, I have to ask you one question."

When first deciding to go through with her plans, Damita didn't expect Dalvin to commit. She knew since he had gotten out of prison, he only wanted to manage the exotic car salon she'd hipped him to, and make up for the lost time he'd missed with his wife, Charmaine.

But, she trusted him with her own life, and she had to hear him tell her no before she considered her other options. In addition, he was expecting a baby.

Dalvin figured she was trying to conjure up an answer. She was too quiet. He interjected.

"Are you sure there's no other way? I mean, her lawyer, what's he saying about her chances?"

She picked up a seashell from the dirt and flung it towards an incoming wave. White froth settled between her toes.

"I'm afraid that's something we can't wait on." She faced him, her look, serious. "You know how the system is, you've been there. The only reason they haven't done anything at this point is the lawyer. He's fighting, trying to get stays and all this other bullshit, but time is running out. All she needs is a technicality, something that'll take the death sentence away. But we running out of time, D. Just last week, her lawyer called and informed me that her second Stay of Execution was denied."

Not saying anything, Dalvin could see the pain etched on Damita's face. He knew about the money, the offshore accounts Yasmina left her. However, there was something he wasn't getting.

Grabbing her hand, he said earnestly, "Cuz, what's the real reason? I know it's not because of what she's done for you. Be real with me, I'm about to put my life on the line, not to mention the fact I have a baby girl on the way."

A tear creased Damita's eye. Wiping it away with the sleeve of her shirt, she began telling him about Serosa.

"I only want to give Yasmina that much. A chance to get to know the child she carried for nine months." A pleading look following, she added, "Doing it through a telephone isn't enough."

Before the two had realized, the course of an hour had elapsed. The murky purplish clouds had long swallowed the sun, and only a purple haze remained. The other couples walking the beach seemed to have vanished.

Standing to the side, gazing out into the vast nothingness of the ocean, Dalvin slipped into a world of thoughts.

There were the many visits, the long trips, and the many miles Charmaine had driven up and down those desolate highways, only to ensure that his duration in prison was comfortable.

As these things played in his mind, he was thankful to have had someone ride with him - someone to laugh, cry, and love. Then Yasmina surfaced. Someone who came through and gave him a chance when he couldn't get one from the people he'd known and hung around most his life. People he'd done dirt with.

The pain he felt was real and the memories of all who'd forgotten him, no letter, commissary, and not even pressing #5 when he called long distance, told of the type of people he once dealt with. However, Yasmina was different, and he could not turn his back on her, he would be turning his back on Damita, and himself.

With his arm draped across Damita's shoulder, the two walked toward the chain of high-rise hotels. Their unspoken silence was filled, there were no doubts.

In Damita's mind, she knew she had someone trustworthy and capable. In Dalvin's, there was someone that would go to the ends of the earth for him, if need be.

Dalvin smirked at the comment made by Kasmir, but it was Shukre who really brought the laughter.

"Damn, son!" Who you jacked without us knowing? Bin Laden?"

The weapon he'd previously had was now discarded, and another was being inspected by him, thoroughly.

"This muthafucka right here!" Shukre said admiringly, as he fingered the triggering mechanism of the grenade launcher. "A nigga betta get some act-right up in'em real fast, 'cause when I come through blasting, ain't gon' be no one alive to tell about it."

Both Dalvin and Kasmir laughed.

"Slow down, partna," Dalvin said snatching the weapon from Shukre's hand. "You'll get your chance real soon, and your ass better not bitch up when shit gets hectic."

Emulating a frightened woman, he said, "Oh my gosh why are they shootin' at us? Dalvin…Kasmir…Please, help me."

This caused laughter to erupt throughout the garage. The only one who didn't laugh was Shukre.

"Oh yeah, we'll see who gets the last laugh!"

Chapter 17
Decisions

Rain sheets blew in hard from the Potomac River. Cold, shivering, Carey and Brittany huddled together. They'd been at a warehouse on D.C.'s Southeast side, hungry and scared, Carey continuously begged Gaietho. However, her pleadings were unanswered.

He was a wreck, pacing back and forth from one distance of the floor to the other. He still wore the same clothing; dark trench coat, dark jeans, and a dingy pair of gym shoes. He fumbled with the silenced 9mm.

Sliding the chamber back, checking the clip, every now and again he would mutter something, and unannounced, Carey seldom picked up a word or two.

Three days had passed and no call from Henry. Gaitheo began to worry.

"Why is he taking so long? He must've defied my orders and contacted the authorities." Quickly glancing at his two hostages, he uttered, "For that, they must die!"

Carey heard this and her heart raced. "I have to do something!"

Hobbling as best as she could beneath the constraints that held her at bay, she managed, "Sir...Mr...whoever you are, please just tell me what it is you want. Is it money? I can get you that. But please talk to me."

Gaietho poised the gun to his head. He was confused.

He knew the Senator was moving against him, but he only needed time. Time would change everything.

Every few seconds his gaze would saunter in Carey's direction. "I need a safe house, something far away from here. Somewhere I can blend in." The words of his mother played in his head again.

"Abdul, no matter what happens, do not let these people change you. Don't become a monster like they are."

Smashing both palms against his head, he cried out, "I can't do this!"

Carey became startled. She watched for minutes as the crazed gunman mumbled incoherently to himself. But his last words, she'd heard. She used this to her advantage, speaking in her most sincere voice.

"Sir, I know you don't want to harm us. Please, let us go. You don't have to have our blood on your hands." Her voice was strained, but she remained determined. "I promise you, we won't go to the authorities."

She'd said too much. Without realizing the volition of her words, when the second 'authorities' left her mouth, Gaietho's head snapped in her direction.

"For your sake," he crossed the small distance, standing directly in her face. "You better hope your husband finds what I want." Shaking his head, he warned, "Going to the police will only cause your death."

The iciness in his delivery frightened Carey. She cast her head to the floor.

Moving away, Gaietho knew letting them live wasn't possible. They'd seen his face. Knew too much.

Henry remained at home, his nerves unsettled. He couldn't sleep, couldn't eat and barely paid attention to his hygiene. In sheer anticipation, he waited for the phone to ring, even though he had Gaietho's number.

The basement was as far as he went. It was sparsely furnished. An old beaten recliner with its leather peeling was used as a bed. A set of golf clubs, two unused exercise bikes collecting dust, a box of tools, Brittany's baby crib, and traces of old memories stashed away in boxes that Carey seldom looked through when she thought of how things were before becoming involved with the government.

Henry never expected the ordinary when it came to doing things. It's the reason he'd hidden the disc in the most obvious place. No one would think to look there.

Now, as he frantically rifled through the cache of boxes, raking, shoving, and placing things aside, he was shocked to find the disc missing,

Nervously, he strummed his fingers against the chair.

A grave thought surfaced. Henry shook his head. "It can't be! He voiced incredulously. 'I know Carey didn't move it."

As the questions came, he tried to justify his motive for removing the disc was right. But the fact remained that Serosa could've damaged him and everything he'd worked for was a determining factor for his actions. It was best to completely delete her from the files. If there was no knowledge that she existed, there could never be a connection; ever.

The phone ringing startled him.

"Hello!" he said, practically out of breath. He'd leaped at the phone.

Silence.

Then, very slightly, but audile enough to be heard, a voice sounded.

It was a tiny whimper, a desperate, muffled cry, but nonetheless inexplicably familiar.

"Britt!" he yelled into the receiver.

A nostalgic yearning crept through Henry's body. His very fears of what could be happening to his family were coming alive. He could hear it in the distant cry. Then came a response.

"Hello!" it was a woman's voice. "Doctor Steven, is that you?"

Henry recoiled, shrinking back into his seat. "How could this be?" he asked himself. "I know I heard Brittany's voice. I know her cry anywhere."

As he tried making sense of everything, he was brought back to reality when the lady mouthed, "This is Shelley from the Human Resources Department. I was informed to contact you. It's been three days and no one's heard anything from you. Is everything alright?"

Henry's head spun. The whirlwind of events were taking its toll, and to have his job harasses him at this point and time didn't help his situation. Gently, he replaced the receiver on the cradle.

The phone rang again.

"Look here damn it!" he cursed, snatching the receiver up. "I don't have to explain why I'm miss…."

"Henry!"

It was that voice again. The man, the person who kidnapped his wife. And to hear the dead tone shocked Henry. But, this man held his family captive, and something had to be done. He replied hesitantly.

"Yes, this is Henry."

"You have what I want, the disc?"

Henry bit down on his nails. "I can't tell him that I can't find it. I have to stall, ask Carey if she somehow moved it."

"First, let me speak to my wife. I want to assure she's alright."

Gaietho thought this to be a bold move. He placed the phone to his chest. Glancing in the direction of Carey, whose eyes were sad but remained hopeful, he started towards her.

"Henry, is that you?" she burst into tears.

Swallowing the lump that had formed in his throat, Henry took control of the situation.

"Carey, honey I need you to listen." It didn't work. She cried harder.

In the background, he could hear both Carey and Brittany sobbing, pleading for him to come to their rescue.

Henry realized that time was of the essence.

"Damn it, Carey! Shut the hell up and listen to me." This time it worked. He continued. "I need to know where you put the disc, the one that was in the box in the basement."

Carey was confused. All sorts of emotions ran through her mind.

"A disc…a God-forsaken disc!" she exclaimed in silence. "Our lives are hanging in the balance and all he can do is ask me about a disc? Is that all he cares about, a god damned disc?" She regained her composure when Henry's voice registered.

"It was in a box that held our old photos, the one of us on our honeymoon in Cancun. I need to know where you put it."

"Bu…but, why is a disc so impor…" she stammered only to be interrupted by Henry.

"God damn it, Carey! The disc is what he's after. If I find it, I can get you and Brittany back home, safely." He was irritated from all the questions.

Henry felt bad. He'd never done as much as raised his voice at his wife. Time was critical and he was only attempting to save their lives.

Carey's mind went into survival mode. She thought back to the day she and Brittany ventured down into the basement.

****

The place was dark and smelled of mildew. Cobwebs were everywhere. Dust thrived on the cold cement walls.

Grabbing hold of the wall railings, Carey and Brittany descended, each step causing the wooden 2x4 planks to creak.

Finally at the bottom, they both looked around the dimly lit space. It was an area they seldom visited. Spotting what she'd come in the basement for, Carey removed the plastic tarp. A box sat under it.

"What's in it, mom?"

Carey pulled out an old picture frame of Henry and herself. "This was taken when we were in college. It was our honeymoon in Cancun, Mexico."

Rummaging further into the bottom of the box, she said, "What's this doing in here?" It was the disc Henry hid months back.

Holding it closer to her eyes, she dusted off the plastic casing. "Um, St Bonaventrues – case file #26847, Serosa Love." A puzzled expression on her face, she looked to Brittany and said, "Classified information, whadaya' say we check it out when we get back upstairs?" she stuffed it in the pocket of her apron.

After brushing the photo album off, she tucked it under her arm. "Let's go kiddo. No telling what's creeping around down here."

A brief smile appeared, only to disappear when hearing Henry say, "Carey the disc, where is it?"

Gaietho was quickly becoming impatient. He'd let the woman talk too long, and there still was no mention of the disc. Luckily for Carey, she noticed this. In one quick breath, she gave Henry the whereabouts, only to have the phone snatched out of her hand.

"I gave you what you want, now the disc."

Henry leaped three steps at a time until he was at the top of the stairwell. It wasn't long before he found himself standing in his study, rummaging through the parcel of discs beside his computer. And there it was.

He breathed a sigh of relief. His heart rate was gradually returning back to normal. Bracing himself, he said, "I have it, but you'll listen to my demands if you want to get your hands on it."

Gaietho seethed.

"This idiot just sealed the fate of his family." He looked back at Carey and Brittany, who now looked somewhat hopeful. But, just as fast as the madness ran through his mind, it subsided. "The disc is my only safe passage…get out of jail free card, the only leverage I have over the Senator."

He listened to reason.

Henry surprised even himself. There were plenty times he wanted to give into the demands, anything to free his family. However, there was the reality that this man could still kill his family with or without the disc. It was a chance he had to take.

"Obviously," he quipped, finding his voice. "This disc is somewhat dear to your own life, or you would've killed them a long time ago. Now, I have something you want and you have something I want."

To make certain that you abide by your word, I've come up with something."

Gaietho was about to protest when Henry interrupted.

"No, you shut up and listen!"

Gaietho smacked the gun against his leg. He remained quiet.

"In an hour, I will ring your number and tell you where you can find the disc. It will be located in a public place, and lots of people will be around. But before I give you that information, my family will have to be released."

"That, I don't agree with. How do I know if I can trust you?"

"That's just it," replied Henry matter of factly. "You don't know. But, I can assure you of this, I would not jeopardize the safety of my family if I didn't intend on honoring the agreement."

Gaietho shook his head. "That won't work, Henry. When I receive the disc, you'll receive your family.'

Henry was about to protest when, Gaietho added, "One hour, not a minute longer."

The line went dead.

Chapter 18
WHAT?

"What? $100,000 dollars!" Leander shouted, his voice echoing throughout the apartment. "My goodness, Benita, I don't have that kind of money."

Benita's eyes fluttered, falling to the floor. In them were something more maligned than hurt, there was evilness, something caused by pain and anguish.

Leander's outburst caught her off guard, ripping her heart into millions of pieces. It wasn't the fact of him informing her about the money, she knew how duplicitous he could be.

Standing in between the doorway of the guest room, she eyed the spacious condo. Pointing, she said, "A cathedral ceiling, imported Italian Leather Corinthian hand made furniture, not to mention crafted in and shipped from, Italy." She slowly moved onto the next item. The kitchen.

Marble floors and walls. "A black onyx island bar. Nice." She swept her hand across the smooth and shiny surface. Continuing she said, "A Sub Zero refrigerator, must've cost a pretty penny. "She looked back at Leander, who trailed her.

"Benita, you're not being fair," he whined. "Everything I have, I've worked damn hard for." She shot him a menacing stare.

She was appalled. "How can he stand here and lie directly to my face?" She wondered incredulously.

Her thoughts were written on her forehead as Leander quipped, "I wouldn't lie to you."

Shaking her head, she said, "The Mercedes, I know it had to cost every bit of $100,000 dollars."

"Hundred forty-five," he chimed simultaneously not letting her depreciate the value.

"Oh, okay, Mr. Big shot!" she sarcastically followed, adding. "For you to be out here living in the lap of luxury, the money's gotta be coming from somewhere." Pausing, she added, "Again, where did you say you work?"

It was Leander's turn to show dismay. For the past few days, since the visit, things had been going wonderful. He'd taken his sister and niece out on the town. They toured the city.

"What more does she expect from me?" he asked himself as Benita stood waiting for his response.

"Where I work isn't what is important." He mouthed, not able to hold eye contact. "You asked for $100,000 dollars and I told you I don't have that kind of money. It's not like you asked for five or ten grand."

Benita had had enough. She tried everything in her will to redirect the anger that was mounting. She couldn't. With a pointed finger, she unleashed a torrent of insults.

"You listen here, you sorry mother...uh!" she cringed in anger, trying to hold back her curse. She continued. "You know what? I'm not going to waste a good curse on your sorry ass. But I will tell you this much." They were face to face. "Before even coming, I figured this much about you. There wasn't ever a time when I turned my back on you, but somehow, you find it very easy to disappoint me when I need your back."

Leander listened, saying nothing.

"To think things had probably changed with you! Who was I fooling? People like you don't change, they get worse. I should've washed my hands off with you a long time ago. "If not for mom and dad," her voice trailed off. "I would've counted you for dead in my life."

Her strong words slammed into him like a bullet. He realized she was coping with something stressful, Chaunna's illness. "Why would she unleash her anger on me when I honestly tell her the truth?"

His thoughts were answered when she said, "You think I don't know about the money?"

His body tensed. "What money?"

"The money mom and dad left you from their insurance policy." She eyed him disdainfully. "You think I don't know about it? You were supposed to divide it with me, but I still haven't received my cut."

He was in a daze. His mind played back the memory of the funeral; sadness engulfed him.

****

The cemetery was packed. Relatives and friends gathered on that overcast day to mourn the tragic loss of their parents. He struggled with tears. It pained his heart to watch the caskets lowered into the ground.

The heart-wrenching sobs and hopeless wailing bombarded his ears. It was his sister, Benita, desperately reaching for the coffins, trying to hold on to the people she loved.

He stood by a tree, too ashamed to show his face, the embarrassment from years before still plaguing him. As Leander's thoughts surfed on that somber day, it wasn't until Benita said, "Oh, now the cat has your tongue!" when he came out of his stupor.

———————

Leander tried to think of something, anything. He said the first thing that came to mind.

"I, ah…used that money on investments."

Her eyes shot daggers at him. "You mean to tell me that you invested $750,000 dollars, half of which was mine, and don't have a hundred thousand to give me to help with Chaunna's medical cost?

Leander said nothing.

She continued." I see where the investment went." She gestured at certain items in the apartment. "Everything I named earlier, the car included, probably was around $200,000. Let me see where else my money went." She headed in the direction of the elevator. Lee followed, like a sick puppy.

"Oh, what do we have here, an elevator! Now, I know the maintenance is costing you a pretty penny. Let's say, five grand a month." Leander was about to object when she threw a hand in the air. "You have a third floor?" she questioned, finding the smaller level. It was hidden behind plastic lining.

Hurriedly, he moved in front of her.

"This is nothing Benita," he tried turning her back in the direction they had come. "I'm having some renovations done up there. It's too dangerous. Let's head back and we can talk in the living room."

Jerking away, she abruptly turned on her heels. "Oh, now you wanna talk? What? You have something in there you don't want me to see?"

Leander raced for the door, only to be pushed aside as Benita moved through the plastic awning.

"What the fuck?" she cursed, as she stared unbelievingly.

She couldn't believe what her eyes were focusing on. Chains, dangling, hanging, from everywhere. Machines, with automatic compressors attached to airlines that were connected to dildos and hooks; Sharp ones, big and small. Posters of men, boys, and babies, all hanging against the wall.

A cold chill sailed down the spine of Benita's back. She felt sick, nauseous. She gagged at the material lying atop a table. Videos, discs, cameras, tape, ropes, handcuffs, leather masks. Of all the items inside the room, the one that made her deposit her breakfast over the carpet were the underwear. A small yellow pair of Sponge Bobs tights with bloodstains, lying atop a cache of discs.

"Sis!" he said, reaching out, only to have his hand swiped away.

"Get... your, don't touch me!" she belted, her scorned look speaking the volumes of anger and disappointment she felt.   She was frustrated. Her larynx tasted of bile rising at the top of her throat. "How could you?" … something like this, Lee?" Tears flooded her eyes. The words wouldn't come.

In one swift movement, she bolted form the room, by passed the elevator, and ran down the stairs with Leander on her trail.

"Please, Benita… just hea…"

Benita wanted no part of it. In her mind, she could've forgiven him for what he'd done in the past - destroying her marriage and spending her money. "But, pedophilia?" She voiced the word in her head. "I can't forgive."

The cab arrived at the airport half an hour later. The moment the plane reached 30,000 feet, Benita looked to assure Chaunna was comfortable.   When satisfied, she fished through her purse until coming to a card. Rochelle DeMarcus. DIVA'S DIVINE HAIR SALON 912-555-2436.

In that brief second, a decision had been made. "I'll take Damita's offer!"

Chapter 19
Once Again, it's on!

"I knew I'd catch yo' ass slippin!"

Startled, Serosa spun on her heels only to find she was cornered. Her mind raced.

"Fuck!" she cursed silently, knowing she shouldn't have come by herself.

Standing a few feet away was Sherry, pulling on a cigarette, thumping the ashes to the floor.

With the small riot being over, the heightened sense of danger still remained, so most were cautious about how they traveled, and where they went. It was advice given to Serosa by Lottie, something she obviously didn't heed.

Upon entering the laundry facility, she'd noted the room was sparsely occupied. A few paired inmates here and there sidling through linen. Her dirty bag flung over her shoulder, she walked past the heavy duty industrial machines that churned noisily.

It wasn't until she'd placed her bag atop the folding table when she caught movement through the reflection of a machine's glass. The few inmates within the room were leaving. Fast.

Sherry kicked the door shut. "Funny how the tables turn, huh bitch?" The anger was written over her face.

Serosa knew she was trapped. Looking from side to side, she searched for any means of escape. The only door was directly behind Sherry.

Slowly, she slid her bag toward her. "Look," she said, heaving an exasperated sigh. "I ain't got time for this shit. What happened in the dining hall is over."

Sherry laughed, "Over! Kendra, you hear this? This bitch has the nerve to tell me it's over."

Serosa was shocked to learn there was another individual. At first, she'd debated on battling it out; quickly realizing she'd forgotten her knife. And now that the odds had doubled, she was aware that the careless decision to come alone was about to cost her, dearly.

Serosa shook terribly, though not visible to the eyes of her enemies. Her hand tucked inside her waistband, she admonished... "Alright then, bitch, if you ready to die bring it on."

Both Sherry and Kendra stared at each other, not knowing what to make of the situation. The look in Serosa's eyes read death, and making an irrational move could mean their lives.

Sherry suddenly whispered in to Kendra's ear, the two separated. Sherry remained blocking the door; while Kendra advanced making her way slowly around the table. Serosa remained defiant in her stance. Feet apart, couched, hand in waistband. Her jaw set, her eyes panned from one woman to the other.

She knew the chances of making it out alive were slim; nevertheless, she planned to fight to the end.

A disquieting strangeness lingered. For seconds, neither Sherry, nor Kendra said anything. Then something strange happened.

"Kendra, get that bitch!" Sherry ordered. "If she had a blade, she would've flashed it by now."

The words weren't out of Sherry's mouth good when she noticed Kendra stumble off balance. Serosa had surprisingly caught her with a quick left hook. However, the woman was humungous, and once she'd wrapped all three hundred-ten pounds around Serosa's young frame, the fight was nearly over.

"Ho, what's the matter?" Sherry teased, watching Serosa struggle to free herself. Removing a blade she'd tucked underneath her shirt, she flashed it before Serosa's face. "Cat got your tongue, now?"

Serosa didn't speak. She couldn't breathe. Kendra's hands were cutting off her airflow.

With the advantage clearly in her favor, Sherry traced the blade over Serosa's skin, coming to a stop when reaching the top button of her shirt. It fell to the floor.

Serosa eyed the ceiling.

"You know," Sherry then added, parting the other remaining buttons, her finger trailing lightly between Serosa's cleavage. "I still have moments when I like to stake my claim on something, or someone as pretty as you." Her eyes roamed over Serosa's exposed juvenile breasts. Continuing, she added, but, from that first day when I laid eyes on you, I knew you'd be a problem. That's okay though!" she firmly gripped Sersoa's nipple between her fingers and squeezed. "I'mma' do something tha's gon' change all of that. And believe me, you gon' like it. Ain't got no choice but to."

Serosa squirmed, trying to free herself as Sherry took her entire breast into her mouth. "When I finish with you, which I'm not sure if I'm gon' let you live, I'mma' get your cute little friend. By the way, where is she? I don't see her running to your rescue. What kind of friend is she?" Kendra burst into laughter.

While the joshing and degradation was taking place, neither Sherry nor Kendra realized the door soundlessly opening. The hum of the huge washers distorted any sound other than what was happening in their vicinity.

Serosa couldn't move. Her shirt was peeled around her waist, a knife pressed against her throat, and Kendra's menacing eyes dared her to flinch.

"Whadaya say we turn this little bitch out, keep her for ourselves?"

Sherry said nothing. She was too busy tugging at Serosa's zipper. Once inside the trousers, she hurriedly parted her panties; her nimble fingers searching for that treasure she knew awaited her.

"You gon' like this, baby!" she viciously rammed a finger inside Serosa.

Serosa cringed, biting her lips as the pain sent a sharp flashing light through her head. In reaction, she hocked spit in Sherry's face, the sticky green mucus smacking her in the center of her mouth.

As Sherry tried recovering, Serosa used the moment to her advantage. She raised her foot as high as she could, bringing it down atop Kendra's ankle with tremendous force. A piercing yelp, followed by a shift in position, allowed Serosa to quickly gain the upper hand. She threw another wild left hook. The punch connected, this time causing Sherry to lose her footing, the blade falling to the floor. Making a dash for it, Serosa managed to grab a hold of it, realizing Kendra was coming in her direction. Fast. Then a thought occurred.

"Why didn't she try to help? I saw her come through the door."

The very thought of being hung out to dry, and abandoned, festered as Serosa thought about the danger she'd placed herself in when coming to the aid of Trish. She then marveled at how emphatically, without any hesitation she subjected herself to the humiliation she was now suffering.

Making it to her feet, Serosa lunged, the blade heading directly for Kendra's neck. Every thought and notion that had existed at one time was abandoned. Only the memory of what she just went through remained fresh. This angered her.

The knife made contact. Blood instantly sprayed, painting the folding table, the glass window of the washer, and Serosa red. Somehow, Kendra remained on her feet.

Knocking the weapon away, she'd managed to wrap Serosa in a death clutch, her strong fingers clinched tightly around Serosa's neck. Then just as quickly as she'd grabbed a hold of Serosa, she released her, falling to the floor, dead.

Serosa coughed and gagged. She fought desperate for air. She couldn't see Sherry clawing for the blood soaked knife on the floor; she just couldn't will her feet to move.

Merely a few inches away, a fanatical expression mirroring a dog infected with rabies across her face, stood Sherry. Her eyes filled with vengeance, she cursed, "You stupid, bitch!" her eyes landing on Kendra, whose body lay contorted in a pool of her own blood. "You should've killed me when you had the chance."

Serosa slowly treaded backwards. If she had ever wanted to have Lottie, or someone by her side, it was now. And it was ever more present when Sherry leaped forward wielding the knife. Everything went black.

Streets are Death Row

PART TWO

Chapter 20
Destination Unclear

The noise was thunderous, the rumble emitting from somewhere around the curve. Serosa's eyes honing in on the large greyhound dog approaching at a fast pace, it was then she would awaken from the deep stupor she had been engrossed in.

Standing, holding a $99 dollar voucher tightly in her grasp, she watched, with no certain destination in mind, as the Greyhound bus approached.

She pillaged through her bag, her eyes cast down, when the unmistakable sound of another vehicle approached, its engine just as monstrous as the bus. A Maserrati Quattroporte stopped just in front of her.

Having been away form society for the last ten years, she eyed the strange looking vehicle and it began to dawn on her how much society had changed. The car's engine revved.

The prolonged sound alone told of the power it exuded. However, it was the beauty of the shiny 22" chrome Sabatini rims glistening in the rays of the early morning's sun that sparked a ray of hope for Serosa.

Besides, her future already looked bleak.

Seconds later, the passenger's suicide door opened…with a hiss. The almost audible sound immediately caused a momentary relapse to occur. Once again, she was back at a time she wanted to forget.

"Serosa," a clean shaven, middle-aged white male, cradling a microphone called out. He was an anchor for Channel 4 News Team, covering what was to be the top story of the year.

Rolling in front of the building for hours, his chance had finally come. Carrying the microphone in one hand and a small device in the other, he was able to maintain step with the two deputies as they escorted Serosa to a waiting van.

She was shackled from the waist down.

Not missing a beat, the reporter asked, "Are you nervous about being transferred to Prag?" his voice quivered from the tedious movement. He continued. "I mean, I know it's an adult facility, and by now, I'm quite sure you've heard the rumor mill surrounding the place."

Serosa was cornered between two huge deputies. She said nothing.

Each time she took a step, the metal bracelet would eat through her bare skin, causing sores to form, despite the discomfort, and she trudged on.

She moved as if she was in some hypnotic state, looking beyond the paparazzi and media hounds that aggressively shoved microphones in her face, and snapped pictures.

A few steps later, she was at the side of the van. The doors parted. The distinct sound, mixed with that of a voice shouting, "Are you just going to stand there?" jolted Serosa out of her dream state.

For seconds, she stared.

Damita sat behind dark Chanel frames, and in the back of her mind, she realized this wasn't going to be easy. Sliding the glasses down her nose, she added, "I'm quite sure you'd rather be in here than back inside that place." She pointed at the prison looming in the background.

Before making the long journey, Damita realized that what lay ahead for her would be a difficult transition; getting someone who knew nothing about her, to trust her. It's the same reason she decided to drive the almost 1,600 miles. This would allow a chance for both she and Serosa to learn a little about each other.

Now, as she patiently awaited Serosa to enter the vehicle, the inevitable was apparent.

Serosa stood with her brow furrowed. "This bitch must be crazy if she thinks I'm getting in there."

Damita noticed her indignation.

Removing the glasses completely from her face, she offered, "Look, Serosa, I'm not here to hurt you. I only came to pick you up. "I'm a friend of your mother, Yasmina."

A perplexed expression shadowed Serosa's face. "How does this bitch know my name? And my mom, what does she know about her?"

Of course, what little Serosa did remember about her mother was vague. Yasmina was a name constantly thrown at her back when she was at St. Bonaventures, and she was punished and tortured because of that name. In all honesty, that name was something she wanted to forget, forever.

Serosa turned away. In the distance, she could see the bus approaching. "For all I know, this bitch could be with those people at St. Bonaventures. Want to make sure I don't expose their little secrets."

As she muttered the thoughts, she impatiently shifted back and forth. Damita noticed this.

Realizing she was running out of time, she laid all of her cards on the table. The bus was now parked, idling. Waiting on a few passengers to board. After all had entered, the driver glanced at Serosa, thumbing his fingers against the steering wheel.

"Are you boarding, miss?"

Damita's ears pricked at hearing this. She waited for an answer. She already played her trump card, revealing it was she who'd paid the corrections officer, Benita to place the shank between her linen. Her only hope now was that Serosa was convinced.

She didn't budge.

Though the words the stranger had told her held significance, the fact remained that Sersoa wasn't impressed. She'd been through too much pain over the years to fall easily to something such as this, and realized the government went to many measures at getting the things they wanted.

The bus sped off in one direction, its distance getting further and further away from the prison. Serosa stared out the window. She knew her ride would be long, wherever her journey took her, but the quietness would allow her to think more about her future. And this strange lady will probably shed some light on things about her family. She blinked away a tear as her thoughts lingered.

Chapter 21
A Jamaican

"Yo, Marquis, what was that about?" asked Brandon, seeing the Bentley creep away from the curve.

"Man, I don't know," he replied, shaking his head in confusion.

"But that ragamuffin was talking some cold shit, something about money, some broad; I think he said she was his granddaughter."

"Well, who was he?" Brandon asked, clearly disturbed. For the last two months, other dealers had been trying to muscle in on his territory. He needed to know who this could be.

"How in the hell do I know?" Marquis replied, clearly agitated.

"All I know is, the one driving was burning some fire as cush...the shit smelled too damn good. The one on the passenger side did all the talking. And the one in the back seat, whoever that mutha fucka was, scared the shit out of me. Duke had blue eyes, and his dreads almost covered his entire body. He was in a wheelchair."

Brandons's mind started racing. He knew the Westside Nobhill Crew didn't pose any danger, they'd come to an agreement months back. Then a thought occurred, "J.T.!" he mouthed aloud, startling Marquis. "I bet it was his doing, having the Jamaicans come through." Looking at Marquis, he added, "I guess he think their presence will make me give him a piece of my block."

For the last two years, Brandon ruled the Pearl District with an iron fist. At such a young age of 20, many wondered how he came to be so powerful in the game. But that power came at a price, a tag that would haunt him for the rest of his days.

The block was NW 21st and Burnside Avenue. The Pearl District was saturated with crack spots, illegal gambling and liquor houses and an array of corners where smack was delivered throughout the night, and in this arena, Brandon was King.

Now, as he sat behind the wheel of the charcoal black Mercedes Benz CL 550-AMG, his mind went back to how he gained sovereignty.

****

Gunfire erupted. The shots alerted everyone to take cover, or become a statistic. When the smoke finally cleared on that warm-sunny day in northwest Portland, two lay dead, and one impeccably dressed for such an occasion, lay in a puddle of his own blood, as he stared death in the face.

Brick was one of the city's largest smack dealers. And for, years, he knew things would eventually play out this way. It was the way of the gangsta.

"You come up in the ranks starting as a runner, then lookout, and so on..." he explained to the two youths that eagerly listened.

Brandon and J.T. were fourteen, and they were hungry for a chance at success, as they listened to Brick give his sermon.

"Everybody can't afford to spend a grip on clothes, bitches, or a nice pad to lay your head at. Only certain few have what it takes to make it in this game. And that's heart, young jits. You gots to have heart!"

Neither Brandon nor J.T., spoke. They both were too mesmerized by the platinum medallion hanging around his neck, the iced-out wrist link dangling from his arm, and the canary yellow 10 carat diamonds in his ears.

In the city of Portland, Brick knew there were too many ways to make money. Pimping, dealing drugs, con games, etc, and, he was fully aware that the two young jits sitting before him wanted the same piece of pie he was eating from.

Since that day, weeks, months, and years had passed. Both Brandon and J.T. had been under Bricks' tutelage, and business was booming. That's when the inevitable happened.

The gunman stood over Brick - his aim poised, the gun a hair trigger away from blasting. Although most in the streets had cleared, finding safety still remained.

Brandon and J.T. were crouched behind the rear end of an SUV. They watched as Tank, a rival of Brick's, walked over the bodies of two of his downed men.

"I guess it's true what they say about you, Brick." He angrily spat, placing his size eleven gators on the open wound in Brick's chest. "You don't have nine lives."

Brick cringed under the pain.

"Fuck you, bitch!" you've always wanted what I have." The words forcefully came. Problem is- you wasn't man enough to take it on your own... had to let two of your bitches die before you showed your face. If you ask me, that's a coward's move."

Tank stood waving the gun in circles. "Yeah, well, what good would it have done if both of us got caught in the crossfire? The way I see things, somebody has to be left to oversee all those millions you got stashed away in that condo across town. And, I'm about to become the executor after I kill your bitch ass." His boisterous laugh sounded throughout the street.

In anger, Brick hocked green-bloody mucus on Tank's trousers.

"That's what I think of marks like you!"

Both Brandon and J.T. came out from behind the expedition. Neither held weapons, but their expressions were of concern. On one hand, their loyalties were with Brick. He was the one putting endless money in their pockets. On the other, there was nothing they could do to stop Tank from killing him.

Now, as all three hovered over Brick, whose mouth leaked blood and his shallow breathing preceded imminent death, a silent pact was formed.

"Look here, young bloods." Tank voiced. "In normal circumstances, with you two being part of his team, I would kill the both of you and have no afterthought. But this one…it's personal between me and this piece of shit here." He pointed to Brick.

There was silence.

"Now, being as though you two are going to be unemployed by the end of the day, I'm offering both of you jobs." His eyes went to Brandon first, then, J.T.

"Brandon!" shouted Brick, wincing as he forced the words out. He was up on one elbow, the material of his silk shirt soaked from blood. "You don't need this game. You have a bright future ahead of you. Leave this shit for people like…" his eyes trailed to Tank, and J.T. who stood directly beside him.

"Oh! What do we have here?" Tank interrupted, his voice holding a tinge of amazement. He turned to J.T.. "I take it; this piece of shit doesn't give a damn about you. I'm quite sure I didn't hear him say those same words to you."

He placed the .44 magnum in J.T.'s hands.

J.T. clutched the big weapon, his fingers settling around the body of metal. He eyed it as if it were a bar of gold boullion.

"J.T!" Brandon quickly mouthed. "WH…What are you thinking, man?" He reached for the weapon only to have J.T. recoil, a far away expression in his eyes.

Seeing this, Brick chimed, "Remember what I told you the day we were at my pad?" he eyed Brandon inquisitively. His gaze was deadpan.

Immediately, Brandon went back to that day. The words said to him were hard to believe. But, now, as he witnessed first-hand the evil of J.T., he realized Brick's words to be true. "J.T. can't be trusted."

His thoughts were abruptly interrupted when J.T. said, "You know, Brick, Tank's right." He inched closer, the barrel never leaving Brick's body.

"I don't know why it took me so long to realize it, but you don't respect me. Shit, after all the dirty shit I've done for you, I still wasn't good enough in your eyes."

Brandon was at a loss for words. He was fully aware of what was about to unfold, and in the back of his mind, he knew if J.T. was so easily influenced to switch his allegiance, then in time, he too would be next.

Three loud shots rang out. Brick was knocked flat against the pavement. He wheezed audibly as the air escaped his lungs. Brandon was on his knees, leaning over the body, his ears close to Brick's mouth. For moments, he remained in that position. Brick was gone, dead.

'What did he tell you, Youngblood?" asked Tank, wanting to know if Brick mentioned anything about his stash.

Brandon said nothing. Casually, he stood eying J.T. contemptuously. His head cast low; he walked away and never looked back, thinking the next bullet would slam into his back.

****

Fuming from anger, Brandon pulled Marquis, aside. "Pull the team together. We gotta have a sit-down to discuss how we're going to deal with that nigga J.T."

Chapter 22
Never Give Up!

"Well, Mrs. Powell," Yasmina's attorney, Jeffery Standridge, stated matter of factly. "Things aren't looking good."

His once freshly pressed grey Hugo Boss suit was now wrinkled. His face was drenched from sweat, and his glasses sat haphazardly on top of the table.

For the last two hours, he and Yasmina had been seated inside the small room. They poured over every aspect of her case, still coming up with the same thing.

Since taking on the high profile case almost ten years ago, it would be the first time the Jewish lawyer sensed defeat in his client.

"Mrs. Powell," he reached a hand out, placing it on top of hers. "You gotta remain strong, you can't give up."

Yasmina slouched in her seat. She was tired and looked haggard, having to deal with this situation. It was stressful. Casting her gaze up, her eyes landing on his, he could read the solemn glare. "She's trodden with grief," he surmised.

Just as soon as his thoughts came, he noticed a tear sliding down her face. And it was that same tear he'd seen from other clients that told a story, one of defeat.

Yasmina found her voice.

"I had a visit from the administration yesterday."

The attorney was livid. "What do you mean you were visited by the administration? Who? Why?"

Shrugging her shoulders, she replied, "It was the warden, and some Senator."

Rearing back in his seat, the attorney sought for answers in his mind as to why she would be receiving visits for the warden, much less, a Senator.

Sifting through paper located in his briefcase, he stopped when he came to a single sheet. He quickly perused it.

"Did they explain the sudden visit?" he asked, placing the page in front of him. He then asked, "What kind of questions did they ask? Did you inform them that you wanted your attorney present?"

The questions came one after another. And his reasons for the barrage of inquiries involved the abuse of a prisoner's rights to be questioned, and or interrogated, without counsel present.

Having had enough, and tired of dealing with the situation, Yasmina flashed a hand. "With all due respect, Mr. Standrige, I truly appreciate everything you're doing, and have done in the past. But, you're not the one going through this. I mean, everyday, continuously, I feel like I'm withering away, slowly.

You can't begin to understand what it's like not to see your child, or for that fact, be haunted by your conscience for things you're not able to do for them."

Her tears flowed freely. Not once did she try and wipe them away. Continuing, she added, "Of course you may think you know what goes on in here, but you see and hear only the things these people want you to know."

The attorney eyed Yasmina with concern. His attempt to raise a question was staunched when she said, "No, let me get this out. I've been holding back too long, it's gotta come. Now, I know I'm the one who put myself in this predicament, but just as much as you fight for my freedom, I know it will never happen. I was only keeping hope alive for my baby, Serosa. In here, I'm reduced to the lowest level a human can possibly imagine, except for death, which isn't too far around the corner.

I'm constantly harassed and abused by the guards. Hell, if they think I'm looking at them wrong, I'm chastised. I'm losing my grasp on time-I've been here so long. The way I measure it, time is like good health. It's taken for granted until it dissolves, then we start to worry about it. But it's too late then." Shaking her head, she finished. "I'm just tired. I told them to go forward with the execution."

For moments, the attorney sat with a bewildered expression. Listening to the heart-wrenching speech caused a lump to form in his throat. He fought back tears. But, he still couldn't understand why she was giving up.

The truth of the matter was obvious. Yasmina was tired of living like a caged animal.

"Look," admonished the attorney. "I can't obviously say I understand what you're going through, but believe me, I sympathize with your situation. In my line of work, I see people, as well as know of people, that are or were in the same position as you. Some are even blessed enough to have their appeals before the courts again. Others aren't as fortunate. "Grabbing hold of her hand again, he added, "What I'm trying to say is, never give up. You have a daughter that's waiting for her mother to home from prison. Serosa's with Damita. She picked her up, yesterday.

This bit of information sent a whirlwind of events coursing through Yasmina's mind. She instantly revisited the day the warden and the Senator stopped through.

****

Their voices echoed off the walls. Inmates locked in their perspective cells knew someone of importance was on the wing. The staff ran around too much, appearing to be engulfed in work. Both men slowly walked the length of the hallway, the Senator leisurely glancing at each cell he passed. He stopped at one in particular.

"The young lady I asked you about earlier when I phoned?" He turned, asking the warden who stood just behind him. "Is this her?"

"Ah, yes, Mr. L'Enfants, that's ah, Mrs. Love, I mean, Yasmina."

The Senator suddenly sensed nervousness about the warden, but shunned the thought.

With his hands out-stretched, palms open, he said, "Well, are you going to just stand there, or are you going to let me in?

Seconds passed as the warden fumbled with his keys.   Witnessing this, Yasmina backed into the corner, making herself as small as she possibly could.

Upon seeing this, the Senator said, "There's no need for that, dear. I'm not here to hurt you." His confused gaze landed on the warden, who sheepishly grinned.

Yasmina didn't move. She remained in that same position.   "Why should I trust him?" she questioned herself. Over the past few years, she'd heard the same thing, only to be taken advantage of time and time again.

Her next move startled him.

"Hey!" the Senator yelled, shocked at what his eyes landed on. "What are you doing? Please, Miss put your clothes back on."

Hearing this somewhat settled Yasmina's nerves.   After introducing himself and withdrawing from the gesture of sex, she let her guard down. She sat on the edge of her bed and listened as he offered his apologies regarding her situation. He went on to say that if it were up to him, there would be no capital punishment.

Yasmina's eyes swollen with tears.   She thought about Serosa, not having a chance at life because of mistakes she'd made herself. And it wasn't until the Senator mentioned Serosa's name when she snapped out her dreamlike state.

"What in the hell did you just say?" Yasmina cursed.

The Senator didn't flinch. His posture became stiff, rigid.

"I said the decision you make today will determine the outcome of your daughter's survival." He stared at Yasmina with an evil glint in his eye. Continuing, he added, "She can either leave prison alive, of course with your help, or, she can and will be carried out in a box. And believe me," he added emphasis to the word, "I have someone on the inside who will make sure it happens."

Yasmina's heart ached. She wondered where the man's compassion disappeared to. The fact that he knew so much about Serosa frightened her. Although she seethed with anger, she wondered why there was such huge interest in her daughter.

The senator had her undivided attention. And knowing this, he informed Yasmina of what it was that he wanted. Listening, opting not to offer any feedback - she knew what she had to do.

****

Now, as she sat before her attorney, it elated Yasmina to learn that Serosa had made it out alive. But what she didn't know was there was a guardian angel watching over Serosa.

Chapter 23
The Switch

1600 block of Pennsylvania Avenue. It was the ideal spot. Henry selected the locale specifically for its view. It sat amongst the watchful eye of select businesses with continuous traffic. It was also situated near one of the world's most beloved historical landmarks, The White House.

Minutes after the conversation had ended between himself and Gaietho, Henry moved about restlessly. The magnitude of which he was up against was enormous, and he knew his margin for error - there was none. Gaietho was clear on what he wanted, and the iciness in which his words came sent shards of icicles through him. He had to stick to the plans.

The 60 quadrant of the city was Henry's first stop. Now on foot, he quickly trekked up and down the block, surveying and searching for anything to assist in what he was about to attempt.

Directly to his left was the entrance for the city's Metro Subway. "That's good," he shook his head while muttering. "It may be useful in my goal." Across from it, no more than half a block away was the 67th precinct. "Not good." He shook his head again, his gaze falling on the Capitol sitting proudly, nestled in between a few other buildings in the distance.

Back in his car, Henry was about to drive pass 16th street NW when a thought occurred. "Lafayette

Square," he said excitedly. "This is in my backyard."
A smile appeared.

Truth is, Lafayette Square served as the center hub for the White House, the Washington Monument, and various other landmarks. It was also headquarters for the C.I.A., F.B.I., N.S.A. and other government agencies.

He walked into a shop on the boulevard.

After purchasing a pair of binoculars, two long-range hand-held radios, a black hooded sweatshirt, and a room at the Hotel Rouge, Henry began implementing his plan.

From his window, he had a clear view up and down 16th street. The White House also could be seen. The twelve foot cast iron gate that surrounded the establishment, as well as the military police donning the M-16 assault rifles stood by the gate. And within the legion of tourists, the Secret Service Agents stood out every now and again as they fingered their earpieces.

Henry removed content after content. One by one, he checked to ensure they worked. Confident of their performance, he began dialing frequencies on the radio. With that accomplished, he packed the articles in a satchel, donned himself in the hooded sweatshirt, and exited the building through the stairwell. He vanished into the scenery of moving pedestrians, unnoticed.

Crossing 15th street, he noticed that traffic had slowed considerably.

Vehicles that had at one time sailed passed, were being guided in another direction. His eyes landed on a one-way street sign on Capitol Street, NW. Confusion began to set in.

He looked over to left, a public telephone booth. He entered. It was empty.

Cautiously, Henry glanced in each direction. When assured that no one was watching, he entered, poised his arms above his head, and slid aside the paneling of the ceiling. He removed the radios, placing one between a plethora of wires. Sliding the casing shut, he exited, making his way back toward 16th street and Pennsylvania Avenue.

The area was still congested. Pat sat atop benches talking; others gawked at the White House sitting in the distance. The remaining few, snapped photos.

He took a seat, then left.

Thirty minutes later, he dialed a number. He was inside an eatery.

Gaietho answered.

"For a moment, I thought you'd abandoned your precious family." His attempt at humor only aided in angering Henry.

"Is my family alright?"

"Of course, why wouldn't they be?" Gaietho replied, adding, "But how things turn out from this point solely depends on you. Now, do you have what I want?"

Nervously, Henry answered, "Yes, but there's been a change in plans."

His heart raced. His breathing became shallow. He was well aware of everything going perfect. There couldn't be any mishaps. He had to take this chance.

Gaietho shook his head. "Henry, that's not how things work. I'm the one calling the shots. I'm the one wh..."

"No!" Henry interrupted. "I'm running the show. And from what I've seen on the disc, you, the Senator, or should I say, the President, and a few other important people, have a lot to lose if this reaches the media. Imagine how many angry people would want vengeance on you? That's why this disc is so important to you, huh?"

Gaietho's silence was confirmation.

'Good," said Henry, continuing. "In a half hour, I expect you to be at a specific phone booth. It's on the corner of 15th street NW. The phone number is 202-555-1768. When it rings, answer it. Thirty minutes. And my friend," he paused adding, "it would be in your best interest that my family isn't hurt."

The line went dead.

From the window of the eatery, Henry watched as traffic passed. Then, a charcoal-gray van stopped in front of the booth. The driver's side door shielded his view.

He dialed a number and was relieved to hear the distinct voice.

After telling Gaietho where to retrieve the radio and what frequency to set the device on, he informed him of further instructions. Gaietho was about to speak when the line went dead in his ears again.

Five minutes later, the radio came to life. Henry exited the establishment, blending with the others on the busy street.

Amongst the gregarious crowd of pedestrians and tourists, he made his way over to a gentleman cradling a bottle inside a brown paper bag. The man reeked of alcohol.

Henry pressed a button.

After directing Gaietho to 16th street, he informed him to slowly make his way over to the replica of the Washington Monument Statue.

"You think I'll let you walk me straight into a trap?" Gaietho hissed.

He realized Henry was trying to lead him into a public place. Problem was; there could be agents, police waiting for him.

After explaining his reasons for the locale, they both agreed to go forward.

Gaietho was focused on any and everyone milling about. At this point, he saw nothing out of the ordinary.

"Okay!" Henry voiced again. "Sitting by the replica of the Washington Monument will be a gentleman wearing a black hooded sweatshirt, holding a bottle in a brown paper bag. Take my wife and daughter there." He sauntered in the direction, cautiously.

Henry watched. He was concealed by a hoard of tourists. He even snapped a few pictures for a family.

He finally got a view of the man who held his family at bay.

Wiping away sweat that had managed to crowd his forehead, he pressed the button.

"Release my family. Let them walk back towards the van."

"Henry, you know I cannot do that." Gaietho answered immediately. He removed the newspaper enough so that Henry could spot the gun.

Watching from not too far, Henry told Gaietho where to find the disc.

"But," he said with strong vigor in his voice, "Release my family at the same time. "He sighed when noticing his family heading in the direction in which they'd come.

Suddenly, from out of nowhere, came commotion. Gaietho and Henry turned to find two gentlemen, one short and burly, the other tall, approaching, fast.

The crowd of tourists all stood wide-mouthed as they witnessed the men brandish weapons. Shots rang out. The beige sedan quickly swept Cary and Brittany into the back seat and sped off.

Gaietho shed his clothing, blending with the crowd who now ran for their lives.

Chapter 24
Counter Measures

"Mr. President, I assure you everything will be fine."

President L'Enfants stared unblinkingly at his new Vice President. He shook his head.

"I can't believe I let you talk me into this idiotic idea of yours. I mean, what does abducting the child and woman from Gaietho have to do with all of this?"

He had been in office as Commander-in-Chief for a month. And though there were obstacles he faced; terrorism, the economy, medical care, the drastic decline in home foreclosures, the fact remained that the disc was still out there. Another problem to add to the already long list. His mind replayed the scene of the screw up.

The grey Chevy van sat idling. The occupant in the driver's seat was shielded by a baseball cap. It covered his face.

Daylight had long passed, and the street in which the warehouse sat, seemed deserted. The location was one chosen as Gaietho searched for an exit. There were three.

After the earlier incident in the park, he was grateful for the training he'd received years back. He was conscious of the dangers involved.

It's the same exact reason he sat perched atop an adjacent building watching the exchange take place later that night.

The two men in the sedan acted too casual. They peered through binoculars, and Gaietho knew from experience this meant someone else was watching from afar. The door of the van opened, followed by a leather shoe making contact with the ground. The torso of the gentleman stood in-between the opened door, wrapped in a full-length black London fog jacket.

The men exited the vehicle.

"Slowly, remove your coat," the shorter of the two barked, his weapon trained on the man. His partner stood just by the car's driver side door. He too trained his weapon on the gentleman.

Armed with his own pair of binoculars, Gaietho scanned the perimeter of the lot. To his astonishment, no one was there. He aimed his high-powered rifle at the trio.

It came as no surprise that after the gentleman handed over the package; he simultaneously crumpled to the ground as he received a bullet to the head.

He watched as the two gentlemen scrambled over to the downed man. In what seemed to be out of haste, they frantically searched his pockets, rifling through the contents of old ink-smeared receipts, gum wrappers, tissue, finally retrieving the note tucked inside the lining of the coat.

Straining his eyes in the darkness, the shorter gunman read line for line.

"I feared something like this would happen, especially after what happened today. As a precaution, I used this man, a decoy, also a civilian, to run interference just in case you and your employer, the President, decided my life wasn't worth living.

Now, since I know you can't be trusted, and my life still hangs in the balance, here are the new rules.

As the agent read the note aloud, he himself couldn't believe the demands. But they were clear; Gaietho left no room to ponder as he threatened to expose the assassination plots on other high ranking diplomatic officials and the merciless killings of civilians ordered by President L'Enfants. Illegal phone and wiretaps conducted to eavesdrop on politicians in the Senate, and forcing illegal sanctions on oil and diamond field corporations by bribery.

The agent's stomach soured. He knew that whatever was on that disc was a matter of personal security, not national, and the quicker he alerted his employer, the sooner they could come up with a contingency plan.

The car screeched violently as it sped off into the night.

Chapter 25
Becoming Acquainted

Serosa twirled her jet black shoulder-length hair around her finger. She lay back against a set of six fluffy pillows. "I could get used to living like this," she thought as she stared at the pink canopy above her head.

A week had passed since her release from prison. And although she hadn't uttered but a few words to Damita, she was still somewhat curious about the strange woman.

The home, a huge mansion hoarding six bedrooms, three baths and a three car garage, sat in a cul-de-sac located in Northeast Portland. The area, once a predominantly African American setting, had undergone the process of gentrification. Now, Georgian, Victorian, and late edition English Renaissance homes populated the affluent area.

The day the Maserrati pulled into the large remote-controlled garage, Serosa mouthed, "Damn, lady! You live here?"

A smile creased Damita's lips as she responded proudly, "Yes, and so do you." The tour of the place was none like she'd ever experienced. At least any she could remember. For the past ten years of her life, she'd been subjected to sleeping in close cramped quarters. Sharing bathrooms and eating back-dated foods that tasted of mold.

To see a Range Rover and Mercedes Benz S class parked in the garage, she realized that whoever Damita was, she had power and money. This only added to the concern of her mother. "What role does this lady play in my mom's life?" she questioned no one in particular, only to be interrupted when Damita barged into the room.

"Damn!" Serosa cursed, her face masked with agitation. "You don't know how to knock!"

Damita was shocked. Recoiling only after returning a menacing stare, she backed out the door. A second passed, followed by a timid knock.

"Who is it?" Serosa asked with a smile plastered on her face.

For seconds, Damita remained silent. She knew this was going to be a grueling process; learning what, when, and how to deal with a teenager again. "But to be cursed out in my own damn home, I'm not having it."

Her thoughts trailed off when hearing Serosa ask, "Are you coming in or what?"

"Look," Damita said clearly upset. "I'm sorry for barging in on you, but let's get one thing straight. I won't tolerate you cursing me in my own damn home. Anyways," she said with her hands on her hips, "I only came to ask if you wanted to go to the mall or something. You've been cramped up in this house all week."

Serosa gave no answer. Sadness came to her eyes as she remembered watching television shows where families went on outings to the mall and various other places.

Damita picked up on the forlorn expression.

"Hey," she ventured, sitting on the corner of the bed. "We don't have to go today. Just let me know if you feel like doing something. Maybe later." She turned to exit the room.

"Yes," Serosa answered her eyes soft as they stared into Damita's. "I mean, I'd like to go...to the mall."

Bergdorf's, Neiman Marcus, and Nordstrom were a few stores they purchased from. Never in Serosa's life had she seen clothes so beautiful.

The dressing room was a mess. Clothing was strewn all over the place. Beaded halter dresses by Sue Wong. Manolo Blahnik sandals and boots, V studded jeans by Versace, Chanel jeans, Prada, Louis Vuitton, Apple Bottom.

With the items sprawled all over, she took item by item, piece by piece, and danced in front of a mirror. Damita smiled.

The image brought back memories-old memories of herself, Yasmina, and the Platinum Chicks; times when they all struggled to make ends meet; times when they all spent money endlessly on clothes, cars and parties.

The recollection caused tears to weld in her eyes. And it was only when Serosa asked, "Ms. Damita...Hey! How does this look?" She came back from that emotional daydream.

She smiled, watching Serosa emulate a model walking the catwalk.

"Dang, girl!" she replied now standing. "You wearing that outfit?" She couldn't help but notice the stark resemblance to Yasmina.

After spending almost fourteen grand on bags, shoes, and clothing, the two went to fill their aching tummies.

The food court was bustling. Every restaurant within the horse shoe structured establishment produced the aroma of some foreign or domestic entrée; Thai, Chinese, Japanese, Italian, and American. Serosa's stomach hungered for them all.

Girls' day on the town was going well. Damita felt good about the progress they'd made thus far, so she sparked more conversation.

"So," she held a piece of Hibachi shrimp in between two chopsticks.

"Did you have fun today?"

Serosa, enjoying the same meal, chowed down on the cuisine. Having placed her chopsticks aside, used the forks of her fingers to scoff down the bite-size fish. She had just wiped her mouth with a paper napkin and was about to answer Damita's question when something captured her attention.

He looked her dead in the eyes. Her heart raced. For moments, she remained frozen. Still. Speechless, she sat in silence. Damita noticed something terribly wrong.

Turning in her seat, she searched, scanning the areas in hopes of finding what had baffled Serosa. She spotted him. He stood six feet or so, roughly weighing 165 lbs. "He's cute." She mouthed to herself, even though he was more than likely half her age. She returned to her normal position only to find Serosa helplessly stupefied.

"Serosa, Serosa!" she quipped, flashing a napkin before her face. Finally coming to, Serosa answered, "Um…what? Did you say something?"

Damita burst into laughter. "That boy had you hypnotized. Let me find out you like him. Better yet," she raised herself out the seat. "I think I'll call him over for you."

Serosa started to blush. She was embarrassed. A hand covering her mouth, she mouthed, "Stop it! I don't even know that boy."

Truthfully, she never knew what it was like to have, or experience feelings for the opposite sex. But, the tingle that sailed through her body the moment their eyes met was undeniable, even though the feeling was new. And it couldn't be denied.

The two had made it just outside the door, heading to the parking lot, when a voice stopped them in their tracks.

"Excuse me." It was the young gentleman. He reached a hand out.

Damita was impressed. She giggled, realizing the brother seem to have manners. She could see why Serosa was charmed.

Moving away, pushing the car full of luggage the length of her Mercedes, she started unloading the bags.

"My name is Brandon." He smiled, shaking Serosa's hand. After chatting for a few, the two exchanged numbers. A brief conversation lasted, but before long, Damita's vehicle pulled off, merging with traffic. That night, after continually glancing at the writing on the note given to her by Brandon, Serosa finally fell asleep with a smile on her face.

Chapter 26
Hard to Fathom

After watching every news channel, desperately hoping, but not wanting to hear dreadful news about his family, Henry shuffled listlessly through his home. Having finally gone to the authorities, it was hard for him to fathom why he'd been treated in such fashion, as he remembered that day in the precinct.

"Okay, Henry," the heavy-set detective with permanent coffee stains etched in his shirt, voiced. "You're telling me that some man… a guy from the Middle East…let's just say, Iraq," his tone held sarcasm as he poked fun at Henry, "abducted your wife and daughter?"

Though his questioning seemed legitimate, Henry couldn't get past the accusatory remarks he made. He'd seen this type of attitude before, and it came from the same type of people he worked around.

Answering, he said," Yes. And the guy had a distinct accent. If you can get a sketch artist in here, I'm almost certain I can give you a rough sketch of him."

The detective raised a hand. "Hold your water, buddy. I say when and what moves around here. And as far as I'm concerned, you're feeding me a bunch of bullshit."

Henry held a perturbed expression.

"Now, you wait a minute, detective Genduski".

"Genarski," the man corrected.

"You just wait a minute before you go accusing me of doing something like that to my family."

He was on his feet, pacing back and forth. He continued.

"I'm simply trying to help the matter by giving you a description or possible lead in my family's abduction. And as I stated earlier, those other men, the two that kidnappd them after the first kidnapper released them, I don't know why or what their reasons were."

"Okay, smart guy - you waltz into my precinct with some farfetched story about your family being kidnapped. However, this alleged abduction happened a week ago. An entire week goes by and nothing. You don't report it to the local cops, the Feds, not anyone..." He furtively eyed Henry as he continued.

"Then, you say that the kidnapper releases your family, only to be kidnapped again, by someone you know nothing about." He paused, adding, "If you ask me, something smells fishy. I mean, put yourself in my shoes."

Trying not to blow a gasket, Henry inhaled a deep breath of air. He released it.

"Look, I know how things may look, and I know how I may sound. But I couldn't jeopardize my family's life. The man said the disc contained significant information about the President, whom he claims is his employer. I think, no, I know," Henry corrected himself, "For a fact that this man killed Dr. Carmichael, the same doctor who worked at St.

Bonaventures Girls Reform School. All of this has to do with the disc."

At the mere mention of the President, the detective's demeanor took on a new twist.

"Did you just say this has something to do with the President?"

Henry shook his head. He was beginning to feel better. But, before he could get another word out, the detective darted for the door and made his way down the corridor.

Chapter 27
Please God!

For the longest while Benita stared out the window. Her thoughts lingered on the sudden turn of events she'd been forced to deal with in the last month. And this brought on tremendous anxieties.

Though she had the money to cover Chaunna's medical cost, she was still overwhelmed by problems.

Only days after leaving Portland, an already frustrated Benita learned of another situation. She'd been replaced at her job. This bit of news shocked her, but before she could find time in her busy schedule to confront her employer, more drastic news surfaced. The call came at a time when she was assailed with bad news. Having so many problems to deal with at one time, she wondered when or if things would get better.

Days earlier, after noticing how unresponsive Chaunna had become, she rushed her to the hospital. For hours, she sat next to her hospital bed, while all sorts of thoughts ran through her mind.

"Why does it have to be my baby, God? Haven't I been cursed enough? What have I done to deserve this punishment?"

With no one to respond to her questions, she turned and faced the window.

Beads of rain pattered against the translucent glass. And watching the clear liquid trickle down the panes suddenly mirrored a reflection of her life down the drain.

It was bad enough she had to resort to breaking the law in order to get the needed money for Chaunna's operation. However, learning that she also had to wait behind seven other patients on a six month waiting list before she could receive a transplant from a donor of the same blood type, sucked what air Benita had left completely out of her lungs.

She was huddled on her knees beside Chaunna's bed about to voice a prayer when her cell phone rang.

Her first thought was to ignore the call. Then for no reason she could find, she answered it.

"Hello."

Those words were the only thing to make it out of her mouth. Listening to the voice on the other end, at that moment, she didn't know how to feel. The caller was a male. A gentleman Benita had never seen before, nor heard of. But, as he relayed the news of Leander's untimely death, she felt a familiarity about him. As soon as the phone call ended, she wondered what Leander's letter could possibly say.

The trip home took exactly twenty five minutes. After removing the sheath of letters that had managed to pile in front of her door, she found the one labeled Leander B Hudson.

The kitchen bar was as far as she made it.

Benita, (sis)
I really don't know how to begin this letter, but I'll start first by saying, I love you. Mere words can't begin to say how sorry I am for the pain I've caused you throughout the years. All I know is, you're my big

sister, the only one I have, and I adore everything about you.

Everything that you are, I wish I could be. But, both you and I know, I could never come close. You are my strength where I am weak. Your life, by far is one that anyone should be appreciative of. The people that find themselves in your presence know they can trust you. Me, I've tried to find that place in this world, but it doesn't seem to exist. Somehow, I manage to screw it up.

I remember you telling me that Chaunna had a rare blood type, O+, I think. I've done some research, as well as had a physical, blood work and all. The results came back clean.

I hope this helps my niece live the life that God has purposed for her. And believe me; she has a very bright future ahead. I also arranged with my attorney that you become the beneficiary of everything I own, the car, condo, my investment...everything.

And lastly, sis, I know I'm not perfect, but I've asked God for forgiveness for all the terrible things I'd done to you, and everyone around me. I'm finally at a point in my life where I'm going to be happy...for once. But first, I need to know that you forgive me. I'll be looking down on you for that answer.

> *Love,*
> *Your little Bro,*
> *Lee*

Benita dabbed at the tears that smeared her cheeks. For the second time in less than a month, she didn't bother to hold them back. And although she'd hated the person her brother had become, never did she wish he'd kill himself.

Now, as she gripped the ink-smeared letter close to her heart, she cast her eyes to the ceiling and mouthed, "You're forgiven, baby. And, I love you, too."

Chapter 28
Everyone Needs Love

"You have a collect call from an inmate, caller state your name." the automated computer operator announced.

Serosa stood motionless. This wasn't the call she was expecting. For weeks, she and Brandon had been chatting, and though she hadn't committed to anything serious, they'd been out together on more than one occasion.

Now, as she stood holding the phone pressed against her ear, that inevitable moment had arrived.

For moments, she remained indecisive. "Should I click off or..." While in the midst of her thoughts, she was vaguely unaware of the operator repeating, press 5 to accept, and 7 to deny. Just as the operator announced the call would be disconnected, Serosa pressed 5.

"Hello? "Yasmina voiced.

No response.

Again she mouthed, "Hello, Damita, it's me, Yasmina.

Serosa tried concealing her agitation. She walked in the direction of the den. Damita smiled, knowing sooner or later, this call would happen.

Ever since picking Serosa up from the prison, she brooded over how to approach the delicate situation. Serosa was old enough to determine who should have a say in her life, so she decided to let things play out by phone. She'd mediate only after Serosa initiated the conversation.

Their eyes met. And for seconds, there was a mutual acknowledgement. Someone had to be the bigger person. Damita removed herself from the equation, making a detour down the hallway.

Appalled by the abrupt reaction, Serosa moved about restlessly. She'd just circled the end table when Yasmina's voiced sounded again.

"Serosa, talk to me, baby, it's mommy."

Serosa fumbled with the rubber antenna, wiping away tears that had bumrushed her cheeks. As quickly as they came, she began to wonder why her emotions were unraveling. She then responded, "Hello."

Yasmina burst into tears the moment she heard the voice.

"Hi, baby." She cried from joy. "You don't know how happy I am to hear your voice…how happy I am knowing you made it out of there…it's just good to hear your voice, baby."

Serosa didn't know what to think. It was good to hear those words - to hear someone, her mother express how much she missed her, but "How can I express feelings to someone I don't know?" she thought as she harped on the question.

Filled with a mixture of resentment and yearning she finally found the voice to ask, "Why did you leave me, mommy?"

The words killed Yasmina. On one hand, she knew not to expect Serosa, a child who hadn't seen nor heard anything from her in the past ten years, to immediately embrace her. Steadying herself, she tried finding the words to convey, as she swallowed the huge lump in her throat.

"Baby, as much as I would like to make an excuse and tell you that I had no control over what happened when you were young, I'm not going to do it." She hesitated, gathering the right words to say. "There were a lot of things in my past I regret doing. Because of the choices I made, we were separated, and I lost you. Had I known then what I know now, I would have never jeopardized my family, much less, you. And I know I can never make up for the lost time, or the sad moments when you desperately needed me to be by your side, but I want you to know that , not one single day has passed that I wasn't thinking about you and praying for your safety. If you only know how much I lo…"

The operator broke the monotony of the heartfelt speech when she abruptly terminated the call. Dropping the phone, Serosa sprinted to her room and buried her face into the pillows as she cried.

Quietly, Damita tipped until she was situated by her door. A soft knock, followed by a twist of the doorknob, she cautiously peered into the room. After finding a corner on the edge of the bed, she methodically kneaded her hands across Serosa's back.

"I know, baby girl,' she uttered, the lump in her own throat burning. "Go ahead, let it out. And when you're ready to talk about it, I'm here."

Removing herself from the bed, she made her way back to the door. Before closing it, she glanced over her shoulder. "I just want you to know, your mom loves you a lot."

Chapter 29
Dear Diary

Today, we reached the room, and that's when my nerves began to act up. I thought to myself, no, I can't go through with it. My legs trembled uncontrollably, my insides churned, and I felt like I was gong to piss on myself.

Brandon and I have been seeing each other constantly for a month now. I really was beginning to feel him a lot. And there isn't too much I can say on relationships, but I can tell you this much. The entire time I was incarcerated, I wondered what it was like to experience passion with a man.

Of course, like any woman would want, I too wanted my first time to be special. Someone I could trust... you know someone who would promise to be there for the long haul. That person would also have to respect me, my needs and my wants. And today, with Brandon, I knew performing the act would cure the curiosity I'd been having for so long.

Brandon was almost twenty-one. I know the age gap seems like a lot, but I really like him. I've never felt this way about any man

There are a number of things I can name about him that I like, some things are still hard to put a finger on, but my female intuition tells me that he's the one. He has his own place. It's not as lavish as my mom's friend, Damita's, but it's also a far cry from normal. He drives a Mercedes AMG, and has another vehicle parked in front of his driveway. And, the brotha's got money. But here's where things get a little complicated, he's a drug dealer.

Now, if my memory serves me correctly, Ms. Damita told me that's the same reason my mom is in prison for the rest of her life, Drugs. But why is she on Death row? There's something she's not telling me.

Anyways, as I was saying before I veered off course. After reaching his bedroom, he led me by the hand over to his bed. And for a second, I could've sworn I detected nervousness coming from him. But, I shunned the thought as the softness of his lips brushed against my neck.

I shuddered. The sensation sent chills racing up and down my spine. I didn't know how to react, but something, I'll call it gravity, propelled me to raise my arm placing it atop his head. I fingered each wave, counting them as I dreamed with my eyes closed.

The warmth of his breath was tantalizing as he sucked on my neck, tormenting me with a desire I couldn't understand. With a slight of his hand, he gently eased my body down to the bed, the look in his eyes, fire. We kissed...heated, long, passionate ones. I cherished his tongue, sucking the sweet tasty saliva. And although I had never done this before, when I felt the heated stimulation reach my breast...nipples throbbing, vagina pulsating, I knew that the inevitable moment had arrived.

He removed my blouse. "Are you scared?" his eyes asked, his voice slightly shaken.

Without answering, I lifted my head, bringing another wet kiss to his mouth. Seconds later, he took my breast into his mouth, taking his time as he suckled each nipple. I cringed. I moaned. He ravaged, pulling each individual nipple with the suction of a vacuum.

The sensation caused moisture to develop between my legs. It was warm. I rubbed my nails roughly across his back, his muscular flesh absorbing each stroke. His suction became stronger. I exploded in hot flashes. "Oh my God!" I never thought a woman could feel this way.

After kissing over my body, Brandon traveled down. He passed my belly button, stopping only when coming to my Umm-huh! You guessed it.

He licked at my protruding knob, his tongue flickering against the softness of my skin. The feeling was pleasurable, driving me to the brink of insanity. I gripped his head...tight, as I grind my hips to the rhythm of his tongue, then it happened...an explosion, seeming to come from the depths of my soul. One moment, I was enjoying the feel of his hot breath as he licked me up and down. The next, I find myself inching away, barely hanging onto the edge of his bed. But I pumped my hips, fiercely. My aggression begged him to douse the raging inferno he'd created.

Realizing this, Brandon penned both my arms to the bed. He entered me, slowly. My mouth pantomimed, no words coming forth. I entwined my fingers in his, rocking slowly, trying to match his speed. Things were cool. The feeling was good. I was still going through the motions of experiencing my first orgasm.

Then, the pain came. The pressure felt like he'd stuck a mini-size baseball bat in me. Each time he stroked, I backed away further and further until I was partially upside down, hanging off the side of the bed. My actions weren't for him to stop, only to slow down. I wanted to enjoy what he was experiencing also.

After a few in and outs, I finally loosened up. This excited him. I couldn't imagine him as more excited then I was until I heard him say, "It's open! It's open!"

This made him go deeper. It made me moan more. Then, it happened again, this time for the both of us. The music we made was beautiful. Together we shared in something special. And as I lay back, recovering from sexual bliss, I began to wonder. "Am I in love? Is this the reason my mom is doomed to spend the rest of her life in prison, possibly dying?" I came out of my stupor when Brandon mouthed, "You know baby that was my first time, too."

****

After writing her most intimate secrets in the diary, Serosa exited the room on her way to Damita's when the telephone rang.

'Hello!" she answered somewhat excited. She'd hoped it was Yasmina calling again. The past few days had allowed her time to think, and she was finally at a point where she wanted to express how glad she felt knowing Yasmina still cared.

"Hey, babe," quipped Brandon, picking up on Serosa's cheerful attitude. "Sounds like you're having a good day"

"I am," She replied, adding, "I was just thinking about you."

They chatted easily with one another. Then, Brandon said, "Check this out. I have some business I have to tie up, and I wondered if you'd like some company a little later?"

Before he could utter another word, she interrupted.

"Why can't you just swing by on your way? I wanna see you now."

As much as he wanted to tell Serosa he'd swing by later, he couldn't. Cupid had already claimed his victim.

"Alright," he gave in. "But I gotta take care of this today. I can't let it pass."

Serosa placed the phone on the receiver, smiling.

******

"Alright, man, I'm here." J.T. gestured, his hands spread apart, "Now what?"

When arriving, Brandon informed Serosa to take a seat at one of the tables if she didn't feel like waiting inside the car. He walked over to Marquis.

"Take Chino and Wop by the restaurant and blend in. Don't hesitate to blast that fool if he gets out of pocket." Grabbing Marquis by the arm, he finished, "You know he ain't rolling alone. So, watch out."

To Brandon's surprise, J.T. arrived alone.

He and J.T. stood face to face.

"Yo son, I tried to steer clear of you after what you done to Brick, but I see that you're not happy with what Tank is giving you. So, you decide to come eat off me, huh?"

A smirk came to J.T.'s face.

"Well, as you perfectly well may already know, Mr. Brandon, Don of the Pearl district." He chuckled at his own words, "This game ain't made for marks like you, so if you can't accept what comes with the territory, you may need to rethink your choice of employment. Besides, Brick would've fallen sooner or later. It's part of the game we play."

Brandon couldn't believe what he was hearing. He'd known J.T. since elementary school, and to see how the game had transformed him into the monster he'd become, he realized sooner or later, they'd face off.

"Is that why you sent your Jamaican friends to squeeze me? Talking 'bout money, and some broad?"

J.T. squinted at the comment. "Nigga, what the fuck is you talkin' bout? I ain't fuckin' with no Jamaicans. Maybe you crossed somebody in the past and the shit is coming back to haunt your ass." He fidgeted with his jacket then added, "Look I tried to respect the friendship we had in the past, that's the only reason I never moved against your bitch ass. But seems to me, you have a bone to pick…still in your feelings about that nigga, Brick, and looking for a reason to avenge his death. If that's what this meeting's about, then let it be known." He whipped a .44 magnum from beneath his coat, the barrel resting beneath Brandon's chin.

Though Serosa sat concealed by the few bushes in the area, she could clearly hear everything. And it was Brandon's reluctance to handle business that caused a deep rage to surface, bringing back fresh memories of the day Trish died.

****

She cradled Trish's head in her arms, desperately trying to stop the bleeding. She used rags, T-shirts from her laundry bag…anything she could get her hands on. The blood still spewed. Trish's jugular was severed.

Serosa's eyes panned around the room, filled with evil rage. She stopped after spotting Kendra sprawled on her back, dead. Her focus then went to Sherry.

From where she now stood, she could see that life still remained. Sherry's chest heaved up and down, panting fast. Her mouth was covered in blood froth; she moved her trembling lips, no words escaping.

Stepping over Kendra's corpse, Serosa stopped just before Sherry. She kneeled. A blade was buried deep into what appeared to be her vagina, another slashed to her neck beneath her carotid artery.

"P.p.please!" Sherry managed to force the words out, her legs trembling involuntarily. "Yo…u, don't have to worry about me. I know a man who can get you out."

Serosa was unsympathetic. "You know what? You don't have to worry about that. I'm going home!" she belted confidently.

The second the words left Serosa's mouth, she grasped the bloody handle of the blade, twisting it. Sherry opened her mouth to scream, only to be smothered by Serosa's hand.

Looking her square in the eyes, Serosa spat, "I'm gonna make sure you never violate another person, again, ever." With a vicious jerk Serosa slid the knife out. Then, the sharp blade proceeded as it sliced through the already opened wound, severing the carotid artery in half.

Now, as she watched J.T. taunt Brandon with the gun to his head, the thought of that day caused her rage to boil over.

****

"Is this what'chu'want, pretty boy?" chided, J.T. tracing the barrel against his face.

Brandon said nothing; he knew any second his boys would come through blazing. But to his and Marquis's surprise, they were apprehended by two federal agents following a tip about the escaped prisoner, Osei Love, he was spotted in the area.

J.T., too caught up in embarrassing his old friend, was unaware as Serosa crept along the riverfront. She was within feet of him when Brandon's eyes grew larger.

Sensing something, and out of sheer instinct, J.T. whirled around, the massive gun ready to fire. He was seconds too late. The blade in Serosa's hand found its mark, embedding deep into his side.

J.T. dropped the gun. Both Brandon and Serosa scrambled for it. And before she could pull the trigger Brandon's hand clutched hers, stopping her finger before it squeezed off an ear shattering round. In the following seconds, J.T. was rounding the corner of the crowded platform as he made his way toward the Aerial Tram Car.

Chapter 30
Overwhelmed

Upon hanging up the phone, Damita pursed her lips. The unfortunate call was from Yasmina's attorney, bad news.

After learning that the courts had once again, relegated his latest appeal, a final one requesting a Stay of Execution, Damita's mind went into overdrive.

"Okay!" she mumbled to herself. "My show's not until tomorrow. I gotta call Dalvin."

The phone rang a third time before she heard a voice.

Speak your mind." He said.

"The plans have changed." She said with urgency in her tone.

"Whoa!" Dalvin quipped, not clearly understanding where she was coming from. "Whatchu' mean…is everything alright?"

"Look, I can't really talk, but, get everything together, and I'll call you when I arrive at the airport tonight." She hung up.

Her next stop was at Serosa's door. She tapped, lightly.

"Come in!" Serosa said aloud.

Entering the room, Damita noticed Serosa was listening to the latest CD by Neo, 'Year of the Gentlemen.' She was also propped against the headboard, a diary wedged in between her legs. She seemed to be in deep thought.

Pardon me, I didn't mean to disturb you." She turned to exit, only to be stopped when Serosa said, "I'm okay. You can hang around for a while."

Taking a seat on the edge of the bed, Damita's eyes indirectly wandered, catching a glimpse of Brandon's name scribbled in the book.

"You really like him, huh?" she eyed Serosa. Not getting an answer, but noticing the smile that suddenly appeared on her face, was adequate enough. Continuing she said, "Well, I know you've been seeing a lot of him lately, but I want you to take your time and get to know him before committing to anything. But, that's not what I came to talk to you about." Serosa's eyebrows rose.

Damita continued.

"I have a hair show that I have to attend in Atlanta. Every year around this time, I sponsor major shows with Bronner Brothers and other salons throughout the United States. And, I was kind of wondering if you could ask Brandon if he'd mind coming over to spend the weekend with you while I'm gone. I just don't want you to be alone, by yourself. I mean...if you don't mind." She said bashfully.

This struck Serosa as odd. Just days before, after Damita had found a blood-stained towel stuffed into the bottom of the clothes hamper, the day in which she'd stabbed J.T. , Damita had given her the third degree about hanging out with Brandon.

However, a slight bit of apprehension in her demeanor, said more than she was revealing and Serosa picked up on it. Smiling, she said, "Yeah, I'm quite sure he wouldn't mind." She immediately cast her eyes away.

"Um-huh!" Damita smiled in return. "It's you who probably wouldn't mind. There just better not be any hanky-panky going on while I'm away. I got cameras all over this place; you never know when I'm watching."

Smiling along with Damita, Serosa thought, "I guess you got an eye full when Brandon went down on me the other day, huh!"

****

Twenty minutes after Damita pulled off in the cab, the phone rang. Serosa was busy prancing before the mirror with the blow-dryer, wasn't aware of the last ring tone until she'd shut the noisy device off. The answering machine clicked.

"Ms. Damita, this is Attorney Standridge, if you can give me a call in the next few hours; I think I may have some good news. It's not 100%, but, there's a good possibility that we may have something. Thank you." The machine clicked off just as Serosa started downstairs.

A door opened.

"Brandon!" Serosa shouted from the top stairwell. "Is that you? You sure did make it here qui…" she froze in her steps as the huge hand clasped over her mouth.

For horrifying seconds, she thought that somehow J.T. had learned where she lived and had come to avenge the move she'd made against him. The light whirl of the motorized wheelchair came into view and the strange man with the dreadlocks covering half his body controlling the vessel, warned of the danger she faced.

The second Shotty Dread's henchman released his grips, a startling shriek escaped her mouth.

"Com down, gal!" Shotty Dread expounded, stopping the chair merely inches away from her body. "Me no wan' hurt you. Me just came to clear a few 'tings up, that's all."

A second henchman started for the stairs.

"Tell me now!" He demanded, his words slow, his tone, icy. "You alone, or is somebody up there?" he gestured with a nod of the head, "Mek it easy and me see dat' no'ting happens to ya."

Serosa nodded. "No one's here." Her voice shook uncontrollably.

The two henchmen had made a quick search of the place and were headed back when the doorbell chimed.

"Answer it," Shotty Dread spat, adding, "But no funny stuff. If me feel something' strange," he raked his hand across his throat, "you wan' live to see tomorrow."

Serosa didn't reply, she moved in silence. Her hands shook terribly. It took everything in her to turn the knob. And as soon as her eyes focused on Brandon, who stood just outside the door smiling, her heart dropped.

Despite herself, she let him enter. And it was when he fixed his mouth to ask, "Baby, what's the ma..." his eyes landed on the three men, the Jamaicans.

"Look man," he belted with agitation and fear clearly etched across his face. "This war is between me and J.T." He glanced in Serosa's direction. "She don't have shit to do with this."

A puzzled look came to Shotty Dread's face, followed by a sinister laugh.

"The boodclot you talkin' bout, Mon!" he shouted. "Me know no'ting 'bout a war. And, if it's over drugs, me got 'nuff cocaine to flood the entire city of Portland." He abruptly wheeled his chair. He now faced Serosa. "Me came 'ere to get her."

Both Serosa and Brandon were horribly confused.

"Why me?" asked Serosa.

Chapter 31
Just My Luck

"You mean to tell me that while you were confronting Brandon, or so you say, and some girl, in full view of the public, not to mention all of the pedestrians on the river front that day, comes from out of nowhere and stabs you with a knife?"

J.T shook his head. He was tired of explaining to the agents. For weeks, they'd been badgering him into giving them something, or someone, or faced the long lengthy sentence before him, alone.

Merely a few days before the confrontation ensued between he and Brandon, he'd found himself in a jam, a routine traffic stop by local law enforcement netted in a two kilo bust of heroin. It was sniffed out by a police dog.

Unbeknownst, that same day, chief Sculea and his partner, agent Wallace, were visiting an office in the local precinct following a lead they'd gotten on the escaped convict, Osei Love.

They began squeezing him.

"I want you to know that whatever information you can assist us in with finding the Jamaican, we'll put in a good word for you." The chief stated.

J.T. was chained to a wooden bench. He watched as others were escorted to holding cells by aggressive officers.

"A good word?" he mouthed incredulously. "Man, if I do decide to help you find this cat, I want more than a good word. I want a legal document drawn up guaranteeing I don't have to do more than five years."

"Do you understand what you are facing?" agent Wallace abruptly snarled. He kneeled before J.T. "Just one kilo of what you were caught with will guarantee a life sentence. You do the math."

At that precise moment, J.T. felt as if the weight of the world had descended upon his shoulders. His thoughts flashed to his girl, Carmen.

"I know that high maintenance ass bitch ain't gon' ride. The minute they lock me away, she'll take my stash and haul ass to the next nigga." He then thought about the streets. "Life...I ain't 'bout to do no fuckin' life for nobody. I deserve to be out this muthafucka like everybody else."

His eyes falling on Chief Sculea, he said, "I don't know anything about some Jamaican, but I'll keep an ear out in the streets. Believe me, if he's making any noise around here, I'll be one of the first to know about it." He paused, his eyes now moving to agent Wallace. "What if I can deliver you a body?"

The agent chuckled. "We don't just want any body. Hell, we have a million pieces of shit drug dealers like you waiting to come in on conspiracy. It's just a matter of rounding them all up."

J.T. smiled, his eyes landing back on the chief.

"I'll talk to somebody with some sense." He shot agent Wallace an irritated look. "Chief," he said, gaining his attention. "What if I give you a body, a dead one?"

After listening for minutes, the chief reiterated. "Son, if you can deliver me a body, I'll see to it that you don't spend one day in anybody's prison."

J.T. was about to speak when agent Wallace interjected, "If you don't deliver, I'll see to it that your black ass rots inside of one of the toughest federal penitentiaries we have. And believe me," he quipped, a slight grin appearing. "The homies will have a field day over your pretty boy ass."

Now, as he sat in his recliner, wincing from the pain on his side, J.T. mouthed, "Yeah, man that's what the fuck happened." He eyed both agents adding, "But, the question that's bothering me is, where in the fuck were you guys at when the shit went down? That crazy ass nigga had the same gun he used in the murder, with him, the .44 Magnum."

Agent Wallace stood to the side shaking his head. He didn't like J.T., or the likes of him. He'd come across many like him, and he knew J.T. was full of it. Then, thoughts of Jaheim came to mind; this angered him even more,

"Chief!" he belted from frustration. "Don't tell me you believe this crock of shit. He's pulling one of the same stunts that piece of shit Jaheim did when we put him on Scorcher. You see where it landed us. Why is it that every brotha dealing drugs think they know it all?" He eyed J.T. adding, "Look atchu, wanna live the good life and be the man, but when we nab your black asses, you wanna tell on everybody, including your momma."

J.T. fumed. And although he knew the agent was right, he was determined not to do life in prison.

"You may be right, brotha!" he spat the word pronouncing the emphasis to it. "But, you chose your career, and I chose mine. Now, the only difference between the two of us is, you work all year, chasing thieves, drug dealers, murderers, whatever, and get what? Fifty thousand a year. Your wife's probably unhappy because you stay gone most of the night. You don't have time to fuck her like she needs to be. And, the only vacation she probably receives is watching your black ass sit in the backyard on a lawn chair drinking a bottle of beer." He watched as the agent fumed. He continued.

"Now me, I gross your yearly income in one day. I take my girl on many vacations throughout the year, I fuck her good, hell, and I even give her an allowance. The house you probably live in, we rent shit like that as a getaway. So, the next time you wanna come at me with that black...brotha bullshit, take a look in the mirror," cause in the end, one way or the other, the white man ends up fucking us both."

Agent Wallace charged J.T.

"Calm down, Wallace." The chief chimed, grabbing hold of his shirt. "We still have a job to do."

After deceivingly giving the agents' Brandon's location, the three packed into the sedan and headed to northeast Portland. But J.T. had other plans in mind.

The sedan pulled onto the corner and parked simultaneously. Both agents noted the expensive house aligning the cul-de-sac.

"You drug dealers live real nice," chimed chief Sculea, as he eyed the Mercedes, the Maserrati and the Land Rover parked in front of the three-car garage.

"Is that Brandon's blue Bentley, also?" asked Agent Wallace, impressed by the luxury vehicle.

J.T. said nothing, he sat in wonderment himself.

After scoping out Brandon, following him to the home where he hung with the same girl who'd stabbed him, he plotted on making his move. But, the agents showing up at his home unannounced spoiled everything.

"Let's go, brotha," chimed agent Wallace as he attempted to open J.T.'s door.

Looking over his shoulder, the chief uttered, "Sit tight, you dimwit. We can't just go barging in on them. We have to have a warrant, something to get us beyond the front door. Let's just sit on them for awhile, run a check on the house, see what we learn. Then, we'll make our move."

Chapter 32
Prison Break

Darkness descended fast. The clouds, at one point during the day were clear, though they held the apparent threat of a torrential downpour. However, one fact still remained; they were in a race against time.

After learning of the abrupt change in Yasmina's case, which now was set to proceed within the next two days, Dalvin insistently went through each detail with his crew. They were seated in the garage.

"Alright," he said pointing a long cylindrical stick at a chart, his eyes landing on Kasmir. You will be positioned here. Be sure to leave your radio on at all times. At exactly five a.m., we'll make our move. The officers should be finishing their counts, and our window of opportunity won't be open for too much longer."

Having taken charge after meeting with Damita that day on the beach, he'd strapped himself with an array of high and low tech equipment; digital cameras, binoculars, notepads, a synchronized stop watch, and a pair of night vision goggles. In the daytime, he drove up and down the long stretch of desolate prison road, photographing the landscape; the angles of shots he would take would be crucial in his method of accomplishing the task.

An entire week had passed, but there still was one vital aspect of the feat not secured, entry.

Donning a beige pair of slacks and a white button down shirt, Dalvin walked through the door of the establishment's human resources office. After speaking with a lady situated behind a desk about employment, it was then he would learn the hours and rotation of the staff, how often the C.O.'s made their rounds inside the establishment, and outside of the perimeter.

Utilizing this information, he walked out the building confident that he'd covered all angles.

Now, as he eyed the eight people gathered in a small area of the garage, he quipped, "As soon as your watch hits 4:50 a.m., you'll put these on." He passed each member a stopwatch, night vision goggles, and a radio. He then walked over to a box that sat in the corner.

"Here are your outfits."

Each person marveled at the ensemble. Black ski mask, black hoodie, an all black jumpsuit, and a Teflon vest. He tossed a small plastic container to Shukre.

"Damn, D!" he retorted, surprised. "You into some deep CIA, FBI, and James Bond government shit." Eyeing the canister, he popped the lid and was about to inhale when Dalvin grabbed his hand.

"Slow 'yo little ass down, nigga. You can't go sniffin' everything you get your hands on. This some serious shit. You ever heard of Chloroform?"

Shukre immediately replaced the top, though he eyed the clear liquid suspiciously.

Feeling confident that he'd gained everyone's attention, Dalvin finished, "At this point, I need each and every one of you to be professional. This ain't the time for jokes and games. In order for us to pull this shit off, and survive without our faces being flashed across every local and national TV screen, we gotta dot every 'I' and cross every 'T.'" "Now," he looked to each man, and the one woman whose expression was stolid. "If you feel you can't go through with this, now's the time to walk through that door." He pointed to the exit, a questioning gaze on his face.

He waited. No one spoke.

Having already paid each individual two hundred grand a piece, Dalvin figured, "If anybody moved toward that door, they would want to live to enjoy the money."

"Good!" he quipped, grabbing his phone, pressing speed dial.

"It's a go," he voiced to the person on the end. "Just be at the rendezvous spot, and we'll handle our end."

The phone went dead.

Chapter 33
Raising the Alarm

He woke up early, pressed the button and listened. There was only one message.

"Jeffrey, this is Harold Mundy of Perry & Dellerman Associates. I'm retuning your call. Me and my partner, Thomas would love to assist you with Mrs. Love's appeal. I think together, we can find something that would aide in getting that denied claim overturned. We'll see you on Monday."

"Although the information was inviting, Attorney Standrige hoped the call was from Damita. There'd been an important discovery he'd learned when he last visited Yasmina, and he wanted to know if she was aware of it.

But the day was still early, and as he stood gazing through the window, a hot cup of coffee in his hand, he'd decided to go forward with his initial notion and filed a new appeal for sexual harassment. "It will at least give me a head start before Harold and Thomas arrive on Monday." He surmised, sipping the hot coffee.

****

A light drizzle was falling. Kasmir sat behind the steering wheel of the utility vehicle straining beneath the flecks of water that impeded his vision. He turned the wipers on for a few seconds.

Looking up through the glass that was now clear, he saw the thick grey fog lying against the silhouette of the huge structure, the prison. An eerie feeling crept over him.

Casing a glance at his watch, he nervously checked his rearview mirror. When confident that no vehicles were approaching from either direction, he pressed the button to his handheld radio. It chirped.

"Yo, this weather is getting bad," he said, watching lightning discharge sharp flashes and streaks of bright light across the skies.

Dalvin also watched. However, his thoughts were different from that of Kasmir's. "This weather may play to our benefit," He surmised, observing the rain flecks patter off his windshield, becoming harder by the second.

Pressing his button, he in turn replied, "Five minutes. We make our move in exactly five minutes."

The eight individuals, including Dalvin himself, arrived in the darkness, hours earlier. He knew in order to gain the advantage, everyone needed to secure their appointed positions early.

Now, as the three vehicles sat hidden amongst a cluster of trees, the bitter smell of sweat wafted up their nostrils.

They waited. They watched. Then, on cue, Dalvin radioed, "Kasmir when you hit the power, we go."

Donned in all black, two men emerged from one vehicle. They both took positions on the ground, concealed by tall grass. They were scattered a hundred yards apart, their high powered rifles trained on the guard towers surrounding the institution.

"We're in position." Both men chimed through the radio.

No sooner than Dalvin received the transmission, two more doors of another vehicle opened simultaneously. They were crouched low, making their way over to the razor-wire fence.

"Ready, on your mark." They transmitted, gripping the huge pair of wire cutters.

Dalvin glanced over at Shukre. "You ready, dawg?"

Eyeing his man, Shukre slid the black ski-mask across his face.

"It's now or never. Let's go get what we came for." His expression held a seriousness Dalvin had never seen.

After giving each other a pound on the fist, they readied their weapons. Dalvin, a silenced Tech-9, and Shukre, a mini AR-15 with the silencer, a hand grenade strapped to his waist, and the bottle of chloroform.

Emerging from their vehicle, Dalvin pressed the button.

"Hit the power, now!"

Already positioned atop the tall light pole, Kasmir was about to disconnect the module attached to the huge and powerful transformer when the lights throughout the entire establishment suddenly trickled off, one by one.

Having made it through the tiny slit in the fence, they followed a muddied footpath that led them to the back door of a building. With quickness, Dalvin removed a plastic cover paper, flicked a penlight on, and browsed the sheet.

Pointing, he said, "That's our building right there."

He led the way to a door.

It was open. Figuring the wind was probably the cause, he cautiously peered into the hallway. It was dark.

As he and Shukre stood-backs against the wall in the piercing darkness, it came as a shock when voices echoed throughout the corridor. Everything fluttered. The whirring of strong wind and rain caused not only the door they'd entered through to flap, but others at adjacent ends of the building to do the same thing.

They weren't able to talk. Sign language was the only exchange they could use, which Dalvin to had painstakingly force Shukre to learn only weeks prior.

Following closely on Dalvin's heel, Shukre tripped on the balls of his feet. From one door to the next he went, gazing from one window to the next.

Most of the inmates lay asleep in their beds, not noticing the flash of light from the pen shining in their faces. And at a closer look, once his eyes became adjusted to the darkness, Dalvin noticed a cell door ajar. He looked to Shukre.

"These doors aren't even locked." He whispered as quietly in his ear as possible.

He heard keys. He then saw a light bouncing up and down the wall.

It was coming closer, but on another wing of the hallway.

"What we gon' do?" Shukre mouthed as his nerves began to rattle. He gripped the trigger of his weapon.

Pointing to the door across from him, Dalvin said, "We gotta get inside until the C.O. makes his rounds."

The discordant jangle of keys bouncing off the C.O.'s leg alerted Dalvin that he was close. They'd managed to slip inside the room of an inmate, but not without fault.

The second they pushed open the door, a hissing sound entered their ears. It was the suction from the wind holding the door bound. And the same noise caused the inmate to stir awake to find two strangers, masked, with what appeared to be guns, standing in her room.

At first glance, she quivered. Her thoughts immediately went back to the many times she'd been violated, continually molested, time and time again by ill-natured C.O.'s, and the warden himself.

Without hesitation, she made a dashing attempt for her desk. Atop sat a black medium size King James Version Bible.

Having hidden her fears for so long, the fear of being raped, it was times such as these when she consulted with two things that gave her comfort, God and the Holy Bible. It wiped away the thought of being defiled. But, she'd had enough.

The huge black book gripped tightly in her hands, she shook vigorously until she felt it drop in the center of her palm. With a vicious swing, the blade caught Dalvin square across the chest.

"Oh shit!" he cursed beneath a whisper. His eyes landed on Shukre who was about to pump a slug into the back of her skull. "No!" Dalvin yelled a bit too loud for his own good. He grasped the barrel of the gun-pointing it to the floor. "She's scared, that's all. Don't hurt her."

He knew he needed to calm her. Slowly, and in a way that he brought his hands out to his side, he looked the frightened woman in the eyes.

A finger to his lips, he whispered, "Look, we're not here to hurt you." He waited to see if she'd understood. Slowly, she began to move, though she hadn't voiced a word. He looked to Shukre.

"Check the door and see how much longer we have before the C.O. arrives."

"Yo, D, we ain't got long, man. He just turned the corner."

Dalvin realized they were running out of time. They'd managed to make it past three doors and still hadn't found the room Yasmina was housed in.

He threw caution to the wind.

Gently placing a hand on the woman's arm, he whispered, "Can you tell me what room Yasmina is in?" the inmate abruptly recoiled.

The blade was still clutched tightly in her grasp, but her hand, at the moment, didn't pose any threat. It rested beside her leg.

He called my name. The inmate sat in silence as she faced the two unmasked intruders.

Dalvin asked again, this time slightly shaking her. 'Her name's Yasmina Love, Could you tell me whe..."

"Dalvin, is that you?" she interrupted, hoping someone would wake her from this terrible dream.

Dalvin flinched, drawing back on his heels. "Yasmina, is that you?"

For seconds, there was silence. Then, all of a sudden, she ran into his arms.

"Oh my God!" she cried, a little too loud. But the tears of joy wouldn't stop. Her sobs bounced off the walls, and they were stifled only when Dalvin pressed his gloved hand across her mouth.

"Shhh!" he placed a finger to his lips. "We gotta be quiet if we're gonna get you outta here alive." However, there was still one problem. The C.O. was two doors away, and he flashed his light through each and every window slit in the door.

Dalvin glanced at his watch, which read 5:10 a.m. He knew they needed to be making an attempt to exit because there were two strikes already against them. The C.O. and daylight were fast approaching.

From what he could tell, the thunder had subsided, but the rain still could be heard as it thudded against the roof top of the building. Something caught his attention.

It was the light. Its beam was bouncing off the windowpane of the room across from Yasmina's. It would be her room next.

"Quickly!" she said, grabbing both men by the arm. "Lie down by the door. Make yourselves as small as possible."

Three seconds hadn't passed when the brightness of the light flashed into her room. Dalvin and Shukre lay huddled atop each other, unseen.

"Lil' darling," mouthed the C.O., his southern drawl greatly pronounced. "I think we have some business to finish." He grabbed hold of the door, pulling it. The hissing of the suction seal breaking caused a smile to cross his face.

"Why don't you just 'sume the position and let me get a quic…"

His words were cut short. His body jerked viciously. He landed in the center of the floor.

"What in God's name is …" the chloroform consumed him, rocking him instantly to sleep.

Both Dalvin and Shukre stood in the middle of the room.

"We need to be getting' outta dodge," Dalvin quipped. But what his eyes landed on next stunned the both of them.

Yasmina frantically worked at removing the C.O.'s trousers. When finally having the rim of his boxers pulled below his waist, resting beneath his hips, she made her way over to the desk.

Removing a jar of Vaseline, she unscrewed the top. With three fingers, she dipped into the think gel, wiping a huge swath between the ass cheeks of the C.O., and then removed his flashlight, rubbing the remaining contents on the base of it. Dalvin winced.

"Watchu' do that for?"

Eyeing Shukre, she smiled.

"When his ass finally awakes, he'll suffer so much psychological trauma thinking he'd been fucked by a flashlight, he will have a severe phobia of flashlights for the rest of his life."

In all honesty, Yasmina wanted him to feel the pain of what they'd done to her for the last ten years, but, she'd had enough. "Being free would be enough pleasure for me." She said as they trekked through the now muddy terrain of the prison yard. "And seeing my baby," she smiled as she hopped into the awaiting vehicle, "will be worth more than all the humiliation I had to suffer through."

Chapter 34
Hard to Believe

"I know," the lady mouthed, kneading the palm of her hand across Yasmina's back. They drove north. "It's hard to believe, huh? And after all these years, you're finally free?" she smiled.

For moments, silence remained. The only sound were the rubber treads of the tires rolling across the pavement at 5:45 a.m. in the morning, and occasionally the hum of a huge transport truck whizzing as it passed by yielding a high speed.

They were heading back up Interstate 95, and as Yasmina sat buckled into her seat, watching the darkness like it was something new, she couldn't help thinking, "Let's just drive until everything bad in my life vanishes, past and all."

But, she knew this to not be the case. A part of her past was now seated beside her, in the driver's seat, and there was no way to avoid it. And as she desperately fought staring in the woman's direction, she couldn't stop the words, "Why help me?" from rolling off her tongue.

It wasn't until the lady placed her hand atop Yasmina's, gripping it firm and voicing, "All you need to know is, you have a lot of people out here who love you. And there's especially one who needs her mom back in her life. Serosa." That is when she realized she had friends who would go to the end of the world for her.

Yasmina was overwhelmed by both contentment and grief. On one hand, she was happy to be free, no longer a prisoner. But on the other hand, she'd begun to realize that she'd caused a lot of people, many who were close to her, a lot of grief. And they were still sticking their necks out for her.

Casting another glance at the lady, she uttered, "But, I'm the reason for your loss...I mean, Murray's dead because of me."

Hearing the words constricted Felicia's throat. She fought hard to hold back the tears. Her finger traced the key chain situated just below the steering wheel.

"Yasmina," she said, removing a photo from the plastic sheaf. "Blaming yourself and beating yourself down for what happened that day isn't going to change things. It isn't going to bring Murray back, nor is it going to do you any good.

Besides, he knew what he was getting into when he decided to take part in the drug game." She paused momentarily then added, "Above that fact, I know in my heart now, just as I knew then, that the love and respect he had for Scorcher, it couldn't have went down any other way." Brief eye contact was shared as she finished. "However, he did leave me something more precious than all the money in the world." She handed Yasmina a photo. "This is Jessica, our beautiful daughter."

The car came to a screeching halt forty-five minutes later. They were in front of an old dilapidated air hanger. Night was quickly turning into day as morning rolled in off the clouds.

At first glance, the place looked desolate, deserted. However, as Yasmina observed Felecia going through a series of signals; flashing the head lights, revving the engine, honking the horn a few times, she knew the place was everything but barren. Then, a shadowy figure emerged.

The car crept slowly into the hanger as two giant doors slid closed behind it. Yasmina stared, wincing through the darkness. When her eyes finally adjusted to the silhouetted figure, she released a harrowing scream of joy, followed by,

"Oh my God! Damita!"

The two embraced in a huge hug. Rocking back and forth. Tears of elation streamed from their eyes.

"I...I...can..." was all Yasmina could utter. She was too overcome by joy.

Damita too, was happy, but she realized time was of the essence.

"As happy as I am that you're out, we gotta assure your safety." Placing both hands against Yasmina's shoulders, she added, "Once we know you're safely away from this place, we can party, exchange pleasantries, and buy out the bar." She smiled finishing, "That'll come later."

The front door of the vehicle slowly parted. And what Yasmina's eyes landed on caused her to stifle a huge sigh.

"That's your ticket to freedom.' Damita expressed smiling, as the light of the Gulf Stream 2 Lear Jet blinked. "And no," she added, "That's not mine. It's rented."

Although she was happy and excited about things, there was one thing still bothering Yasmina, and she asked, "What about my baby...Serosa?"

"She's fine." Damita replied. "Once we know that things are okay with you, I'll arrange how and where you will meet."

Yasmina was about to protest when Damita placed a hand in the air.

"It has to be this way, Yas. The Feds, and every government agency in the United States, will be knocking on my door inquiring about you when I arrive home today. Not to mention, they'll be watching every move Serosa makes. But, once I show them this," she removed a few papers and an airline receipt from inside a bag, then added, "My alibi will be set." She handed Yasmina a separate package.

"What's this?"

"This is your new identity. You have a passport, visa, and numbers to a new account I have set up for you."

Yasmina didn't look too convinced.

"Trust me," Damita said with an ominous expression on her face. "I've gotten you this far, haven't I?"

Chapter 35
Wrong Place

Both, Chief Sculea and Agent Wallace had had enough. They'd been staking out the residence of Rochelle DaMarcus and hadn't seen movement for hours.

"Whadaya' say we just walk up to the door and knock?" agent Wallace quipped, tired of playing the waiting game. "You already have the warrant."

His gut instincts were telling him that something wasn't right. "All of the extravagant vehicles parked in the drive way, there's probably a drug deal going down right under our noses." He presumed, agitated by his superior's reluctance.

The chief didn't budge.

"I'm not acting on this warrant until I at least verify that Brandon is inside the house. And frankly, I'm not too convinced by his information." He glanced over at J.T. who rested his head against the seat.

Agent Wallace fumed. Having run the name and address through N.C.I.C., the name Rochelle DeMarcus came back clean. No priors. Never had a run-in with the law. Nothing. And nothing came back on Brandon either.

"Just sit tight and be patient." The chief scolded, adding.

"If he's in there, he'll come out, sooner or later."

Their lucky break came sooner than expected.

Her Jimmy Choo's were the first thing they'd noticed. As soon as her feet made contact with the ground, their eyes honed in on her silky bronze skin.

Agent Wallace was first to speak.

"Man, she gorgeous!" he turned, eyeing J.T. "Is that Brandon's woman, or wifey, as you brothas like to say?" she was standing just outside the cab driver's window.

J.T. made an annoying sucking sound with his mouth. He too wondered who this woman was as he watched her tip the driver.

She wore a beige sleeveless Prada blouse, and a black knee-length skirt that pronounced her curvaceous body. A beige silk scarf was draped around her neck.

She was smiling as she walked toward the house carrying an all-black leather briefcase in her hand. As she fished through her shoulder bag, J.T.'s mind began to work. "Who is this bitch?" he asked himself as he thought back to Brandon's family.

"It can't be his sister, Regina." he said to himself. "Damn!" he cursed in silence. "Whoever that bitch is, shorty is a ten."

Before he could think to say anything else, Chief Sculea chimed, "I take it that's Ms. DeMarcus. "He watched her insert a key into the door. He then eyed J.T. and said, "And you say this Brandon kid, he's the one responsible for the murder of, Bruce Fenner aka Brick?"

The two held eye contact. J.T. nodded only when Chief Sculea turned to watch the woman enter the home.

"He was my supplier also. That's the reason I'm fucked up now with my damn side all cut up. I was short on some dough I owed 'em, so I guess he felt killing me would be payment," J.T. added, trying hard to convince the chief.

The chief glanced at his partner. "Lets go see if Ms. DeMarcus knows Brandon, or at least can point a finger to where he's at."

Agent Wallace checked his weapon. But, what happened next surprised not only the chief, but J.T. also.

"Hey man, watchu' doing? J.T. belted, as the agent cuffed him to the door.

"The chief glanced at his partner and chimed, "I'm making sure your slick ass stays here while we're in there doing our jobs." He eyed J.T. suspiciously, then added, "What, you expect a brotha to just trust your word? Besides, if this doesn't prove to be what you say it is, it's your black ass that will be charged for all of this, since you know so much about it."

****

It was hard, virtually impossible to maintain her composure. Damita remained frozen, unable to move, her hand holding firm on the doorknob. Her mind raced as she wondered, "How did he find me?" then it dawned on her. "The phone call, It was him!" she heard a frightening sign.

Those thoughts clouded her judgment a second too long.

"Let's go!" barked the gunman with the long dreadlocks. He urged her forward at gun point. "To da' kitchen…go!"

The house was agonizingly calm, too calm for Damita as her mind began to wander. Reluctantly leading the way, she seethed as she felt the gunman undressing her with his eyes. It's when she noticed the duct tape and the small spatters of blood which meant one thing. Especially when dealing with the man who sat in the wheelchair. A man she'd heard so many gruesome stories about.

Then she heard a sound. It was barely discernible, but nonetheless, distinct enough for her to realize. It was Serosa.

She bolted for the kitchen. "Serosa!" Once making it inside, she mouthed, "Oh my God!" immediately falling to her knees, crawling over to Serosa whose tears had dried on her face." Are you hurt, baby?" she searched across Serosa's body to see where the blood leaked from.

Shotty Dread shot her a venomous look. Her eyes immediately looked to Brandon, whose eyelid was swollen shut, his bottom lip bloody.

She went into a raging fit.

"Look here you muthafuckas!" she cursed, wringing away from the gunman. Her eyes were locked onto Shotty Dreads. "I don't know what it is you want with two kids, but you crossed the line when you put your hands on her…and him." She said, eyeing Brandon.

Shotty Dread watched the woman, the entire time flattered by her bravery.

"You know," he stated nonchalantly, wheeling the chair to a point where he was now beside her. He continued, "If mi 'wan to hurt the young boy or gal, mi could have and there's no'ting you could do 'bout it. Back in mi days, mi kill you for insultin' mi the way you just did."

The iciness in his tone left no doubt that he meant what he was saying. And, it was then that she remembered Yasmina telling her about how he didn't hesitate when murdering Selena, or her grandmother, Rosa. She calmed herself.

"Alright then," she quipped, finding both Serosa and Brandon staring at her. "If you didn't come to hurt anyone, why is his mouth bleeding and eye swollen?"

Before he could answer, she added, "And why are you here?"

The silence rendered inside the kitchen after Shotty Dread's response, told of the shock everyone felt. But, that moment of surprise would be short-lived when men wielding guns, rushed in.

Chapter 36
Wrong Time

With the way things were playing out, Damita could only hope that Yasmina arrived at her destination safely.

She was still reeling from the shocking news shared by Shotty Dread, and mere seconds hadn't elapsed when she picked the phone up dialing a contact number for Yasmina when someone bum rushed the front door.

Unaware that they were being watched, the chief and his partner stood on opposite sides of the door.

"It's cracked open." Agent Wallace said, eyeing the chief.

Prior experience told both agents that this wasn't a good situation. Any false move or insulting comment could cause injury or possible death, and it wasn't until Agent Wallace's eyes landed on the duct tape, the bloodied specks of carpet, and the huge blade, a machete.

"We need to make entry." He whispered his voice anxious. "You see that?" he pointed to the contents.

Eyeing the material, the chief was about to radio in for back up when they overheard what appeared to be cursing and crying. However, agent Wallace's abrupt entrance through the door put a halt to any of that. He had to have his partner's back.

"Freeze!" Agent Wallace barked, his adrenaline at an all time high. He was crouched low, inching his way toward the two men, his gun trained on the Jamaican with the long dreads that held a weapon in his hands.

The place was quiet. Every bit of sound voided.

Emotions ran high. Serosa, Damita and Brandon, who once feared for their lives, watched the stand-off.

"Ras clot, Sheriff John Brown!" Shotty Dread voiced, the evilness and rage spewing from his words informing of the hatred he held for law enforcement. He eyed the chief. "You tink me gwan let you walk out'ere alive, eh?"

Both agents tightened their grips around their weapons. Each swallowed the huge lumps forming in their throats.

"Osei Love," the chief stated, finally finding his voice. "I'm chief Sculea, a Federal Agent," he slowly reached inside his shirt retrieving a badge connected to a chain. He added, "I'm placing you under arrest, taking you back into custody."

Shotty dread let out an incredulous laugh.

"You're dis, mon?" he shot a glance to his trusted henchman. "Dis' bumbo clot sheriff say he gwan tek'me back into custody, prison." The dreadlocked Rasta laughed.

While the one-sided conversation ensued, agent Wallace stood confused. He shot his partner a quick glance, and his reluctance to realize that the escaped convict/murder/drug kingpin, was sitting right before him, he'd momentarily forgotten their reason for being in Portland. Until...

The second henchman crept as stealthily as he could. He was crouched behind a wall unit near the stairwell.

Having finished making his rounds on the second level of the home, he'd made his way to the basement moments before the agents made their way to the front door of the home.

He could hear the exchange, and it was clear to him when hearing the chief state he was a Federal agent. He made eye contact with Shotty Dread.

Whirling his chair directly in front of the chief, Shotty Dread spat, "Mi not gwan back to prison. Mi rather die, tekken' you wid' mi before mi let da blood clot animal."

Not seconds after the words left his mouth, a loud booming sound exploded throughout the room. The chief immediately turned on his heels to find his partner spiraling to the floor. Blood and grey brain matter painted the floor surface beneath him red.

He was distraught. His mind wouldn't allow him to think. He had no strength to pull the trigger. And now that he eyed the third man, he couldn't remember if he or his partner secured the perimeter before going straight for the kitchen.

It was then Shotty Dread expounded, "I shot da Sheriff, but I didn't shoot the deputy," that the chief knew their one major mistake would cost him.

Dropping his gun to the floor, he thought, "I'm in the wrong place, at the wrong time."

The gunshot sent him spiraling down to the floor, beside his partner.

Stay Tuned For The Next Episode...

STICK & MOVE III

'The city couldn't have been more beautiful," she thought as she stood against the terrace staring into the vast distance of lights. "How did my life become so complicated?" she questioned, her mind drifting back to what led them to this point.

The brink of a month was closing, and even though the beautiful European countryside offered so much, the mere though of not being able to share these moments with the one person she had been longing for most of her life, brought on tremendous sadness. It wasn't until a hand rested gently on her back when Serosa came out of her stupor.

"Baby, what's wrong?" Brandon asked, sensing the trite mood. He then added, "You would think that being in such a beautiful place as this would bring happiness;" he embraced her from behind." But, I can see this is not the case." Brushing against her neck with small kisses, he ground against her body revealing the romantic mood he was in.

Abruptly, she whirled from his embrace, heading back through the foyer that led into their spacious suite.

"I'm sorry." Serosa said as Brandon knelt before her. She was seated on the edge of the bed. "It's not you. I mean, we've been cooped up in this city for weeks. How much longer are we going to have to wait?"

Brandon grabbed both of her hands. "Look," he eyed her without blinking. "I can't sit here and pretend to know what you're going through, 'cause I don't. All I know is I'm here with you no matter what happens. And there's a lot at stake for all of us, your mom, Damita, you and me. But, I can assure you of one thing. Everything that's happened in Portland is behind us now. We have to move past it and focus on getting prepared to see your mom. It'll be soon. Don't worry."

Just then, a distant siren wailed. They were twelve stories high, and the continuous sound of more sirens approaching was clear. They both bolted for the terrace.

What Brandon's eye landed on below caused caution to seep into his mind. Throughout the entire time they'd been at the hotel, not once did they hear the shrilling sound, except for on TV, but now, as they watched commotion below; police placing barricades around the square block surrounding the hotel, others forcing bystanders away, and people scrambling about frantically, he soon realized their troubles and somehow managed to find them.

"Brandon!" Serosa shouted, realizing that whatever the commotion was below, had rendered him seriously disheveled. She tugged at his shirt.

"Uh, what? Did you say something, baby?" he looked confused.

After taking a look herself, Serosa said, "Damn! What's going on down there? It's a lot of police. You think..." she eyed him questioningly, his absence to answer her question shedding light on his

thoughts.   He suddenly made a dash for the room.
Grabbing his cell phone, he pressed a series of numbers
that were written on a piece of paper, he waited.

While he impatiently rocked back and forth on
his heels, Serosa watched as two men in suits, one
white male, the other black, exit a vehicle driven by an
escort.

She observed the white gentleman pointing out
specific areas as officers rushed to the locations.
There was a startling familiarity about them.

"Brandon!" she called, not bothering to look
back.   When she realized he hadn't heard her, she
belted, "Baby, com'ere, you gotta see this!"

Brandon had tried the number twice not getting
any response.   His patience was running thin and
nerves were shot. He tossed the phone to the bed.

After gazing down where everything was
occurring, he mouthed, "What the heck is going on?"
he then eyed Serosa and said, "We need to be getting'
the fuck outta' dodge." His eyes landing on the two
men, he attempted to mouth to speak, only to be
interrupted as Serosa said, "I know, that's why I was
calling you. I thought they were...dead."

The spacious room, all of a sudden seemed to
become claustrophobic.   There seemed not to be
enough space as they bumped into each other packing
what belongings they could.

"Just throw what you can into that bag.
"Brandon pointed to a medium-sized carry-on situated
beside the bed. "We need to lose anything that could
be traced back to us. Receipts, paper, whatever. Just
get rid of them.

While in their moment of panic, they clearly could hear doors along the hallway, opening and closing. And every second or so, a voice would utter words.

Brandon tipped as quietly as he could until his ear was to the door. Turning his head, he pressed his eye against the peephole.

"Damn!" he cursed silently, but loud enough to startle Serosa.

"What's wrong, baby?" she asked, fear beginning to shroud her.

"They moving everybody on the floor out, 'cept us."

"Whatchu' just say?" she belted though she'd heard him the first time.

"Shhh!" he pressed a finger to his lips, moving in her direction.

"They standing a couple doors down, 'bout ten of 'em. The guys in the suits are four doors away."

Serosa began to feel queasy.

"What's wrong?" Brandon asked, observing the abrupt jerking movements of her body.

"I feel like I'm gon' vomit."

He quickly moved to her side. He had to keep her quiet.

"If we're quiet, they won't think anyone's in the room. Can you make it to the terr…?"

The loud ringing of her phone startled him, followed by an intense banging sound coming from the door.

The phone rang again.

A third time.

The hotels' room phone began to ring also. A red light flashed.

Serosa stood bowed on the terrace, her body jerking each time she deposited the contents of her stomach below.

"We know you are in there!" a voice shouted, followed by dull strikes against a door.

The cell phone and room phone rang continuously.

Having finished vomiting, Serosa ran to Brandon's side. "What're we gon' do?"

For the first time since fleeing their troubles, Brandon sensed fear in Serosa. This frightened him. And while he stood lost in the moment, it wasn't until the loud crashing sound of the door being smashed off its hinges, erased his thoughts.

****

The safe house brought abrupt unpleasant memories, ones Yamina wanted to forget altogether. And as she stared out of the dust-cast windows, the panes concentrated with years of dirt build up, she couldn't help shaking her head and smiling. "It's better than being locked away in a cell." She'd muttered to no one particular.

Eyeing a piece of fabric sitting in a corner, she grabbed the cloth and began wiping at the window. Rue De Berne was the first thing her eyes focused on.

The long strip ran up and down the block for

as long as the eyes could see. But what caught Yasmina's attention were the people. Prostitutes, addicts, pimps, all who traversed to and from the seedy street conducted some sort of illegal activity.

And upon learning that she'd be hiding in Europe for a few days or weeks, a smile came to her face. But, reality had quickly set in as the place which she viewed to be an oasis of serenity. It held a stark contrast to the many inner cities in the U.S. and Jamaica, where she'd lived in at one time in her life. They were impoverished, abandoned, and most of all, forgotten.

Then she heard voices outside her room door. This caused her to stifle her breathing.

"Where is the rest of the money, you bitch?" Yasmina tensed.

(Qui est la?)

Though the gentleman's European accent was very pronounced, she was able to make out most of the words. Having studied French I and II in high school, Yasmina was able to discern much of the rhetoric. That and the man used tidbits of English every so often. This led her to wonder who was on the receiving end of the derogatory blasphemy, and her uncertainty was answered when she heard the voice of a young girl he refused to pay. He said I didn't succeed in pleasuring him, and he would speak with you about it."

Yasmina stared at the exchange through the peephole...it ached her heart to watch the girl cower as the man threatened to strike her with his hand. But, there was nothing she could do. She was on the run hiding out in a foreign country and needed to remain as inconspicuous as possible.

Yasmina noted that the man wore a red waist-length leather jacket, a plaid button- down shirt which exposed the Cuban link matted against his thick chest hairs, and a pair of brown leather shoes. "A pimp!" she surmised in her mind. Having heard enough, she was about to return to her bed when something caused her to suddenly stop. The loud smacking sound etched through the wooden door when Yasmina turned on her heels. She found the girl lying on the floor, blood curling her lips, tears dripping from her swollen and beaten eyes. Immediately, Serosa came to mind. And this caused tears to drip from Yasmina's eyes. She could only imagine what Serosa had suffered in the last ten years. Her mind suddenly drifted back to her arrival.

A NOVEL FROM THE BESTSELLING AUTHOR OF "MEETING MISS RIGHT" AND "SEXUAL EXPLOITS OF A NYMPHO"

REVISED EDITION

Neglected SOULS

"Dark alleys, cold and lonely nights just trying to survive... Who can you run to? Neglected Souls made me gasp and grip my heart."
—KaShamba Williams, Best Selling Author of Driven and At The Court's Mercy.

RICHARD JEANTY

Motherhood and the trials of loving too hard and not enough frame this story...The realism of these characters will bring tears to your spirit as you discover the hero in the villain you never saw coming...

In Stores!!

Jimmy and Nina continue to feel a void in their lives because they haven't a clue about their genealogical make-up. Jimmy falls victims to a life threatening illness and only the right organ donor can save his life. Will the donor be the bridge to reconnect Jimmy and Nina to their biological family? Will Nina be the strength for her brother in his time of need? Will they ever find out what really happened to their mother?

In Stores!!!

Betrayal, lust, lies, murder, deception, sex and tainted love frame this story... Julian Stevens lacks the ambition and freak ability that Miko looks for in a man, but she married him despite his flaws to spite an ex-boyfriend. When Miko least expects it, the old boyfriend shows up and ready to sweep her off her feet again. While Miko's doing her own thing, Julian is determined to become everything Miko ever wanted in a man and more, but will he go to extreme lengths to prove he's worthy of Miko's love? Julian Stevens soon finds out that he's capable of being more than he could ever imagine as he embarks on a journey that will change his life forever.

In Stores!!

The police in New York and other major cities around the country are increasingly victimizing black men. The violence has escalated to deadly force, most of the time without justification. In this controversial book, noted author Richard Jeanty, tackles the problem of police brutality and the unfair treatment of Black men at the hands of police in New York City and the rest of the country. The conflict between the Police and Black men will continue on a downward spiral until the mayors of every city hold accountable the members of their police force who use unnecessary deadly force against unarmed victims.

In Stores!!

Just when Darren thinks his relationship with Tina is flourishing, there is yet another hurdle on the road hindering their bliss. Tina saw a therapist for months to deal with her sexual addiction, but now Darren is wondering if she was ever treated completely. Darren has not been taking care of home and Tina's frustrated and agrees to a break-up with Darren. Will Darren lose Tina for good? Will Tina ever realize that Darren is the best man for her?

In Stores!!

Ronald Murphy was a player all his life until he and his best friend, Myles, met the women of their dreams during a brief vacation in South Beach, Florida. Sexual Jeopardy is story of trust, betrayal, forgiveness, friendship, hope and HIV.

In Stores!!!

Tina develops an insatiable sexual appetite very early in life. She only loves her boyfriend, Darren, but he's too far away in college to satisfy her sexual needs.

Tina decides to get buck wild away in college

Will her sexual trysts jeopardize the lives of the men in her life?

In Stores!!!

RICHARD JEANTY

INTRODUCES

Me & Mrs. Jones

A NOVEL BY
K.M. THOMPSON

Faith Jones, a woman in her mid-thirties, has given up on ever finding love again until she met her son's best friend, Darius. Faith Jones is walking a thin line of betrayal against her son for the love of Darius. Will Faith allow her emotions to outweigh her common sense?

In Stores!!!

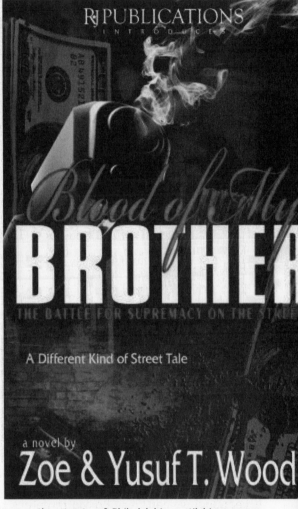

Roc was the man on the streets of Philadelphia, until his younger brother decided it was time to become his own man by wreaking havoc on Roc's crew without any regards for the blood relation they share. Drug, murder, mayhem and the pursuit of happiness can lead to deadly consequences. This story can only be told by a person who has lived it.

In Stores!!!

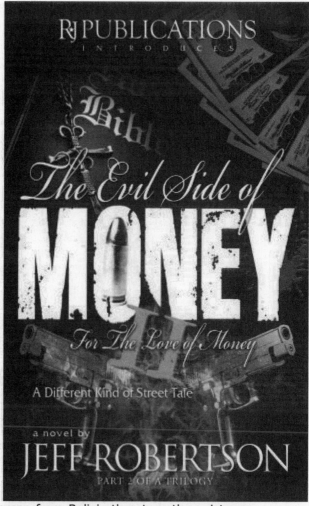

A beautigul woman from Bolivia threatens the existence of the drug empire that Nate and G have built. While Nate is head over heels for her, G can see right through her. As she brings on more conflict between the crew, G sets out to show Nate exactly who she is before she brings about their demise.

In Stores!!

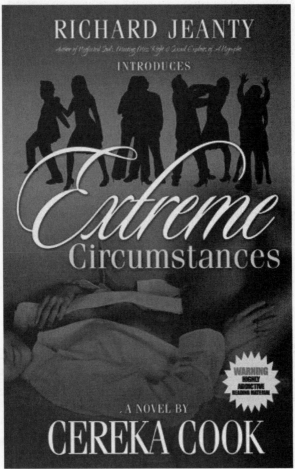

What happens when a devoted woman is betrayed? Come take a ride with Chanel as she takes her boyfriend, Donnell, to circumstances beyond belief after he betrays her trust with his endless infidelities. How long can Chanel's friend, Janai, use her looks to get what she wants from men before it catches up to her? Find out as Janai's gold-digging ways catch up with and she has to face the consequences of her extreme actions.

In Stores!!!

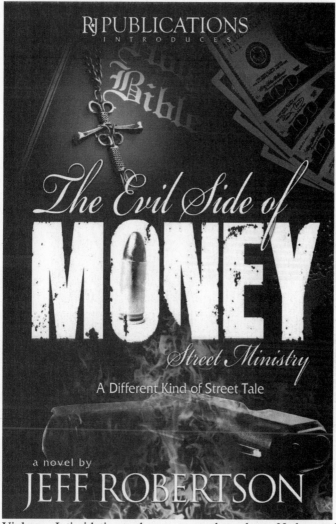

RJ PUBLICATIONS
INTRODUCES

The Evil Side of
MONEY
Street Ministry
A Different Kind of Street Tale

a novel by
JEFF ROBERTSON

Violence, Intimidation and carnage are the order as Nathan and his brother set out to build the most powerful drug empires in Chicago. However, when God comes knocking, Nathan's conscience starts to surface. Will his haunted criminal past get the best of him?

In Stores!!

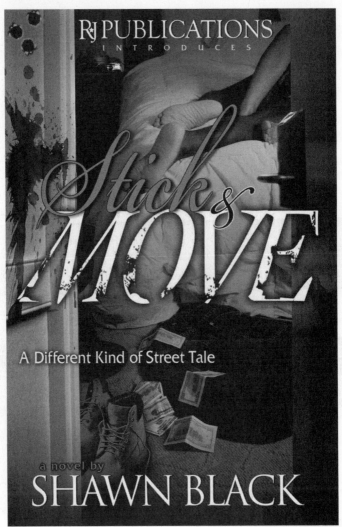

RJ PUBLICATIONS
INTRODUCES

Stick & MOVE

A Different Kind of Street Tale

a novel by
SHAWN BLACK

Yasmina witnessed the brutal murder of her parents at a young age at the hand of a drug dealer. This event stained her mind and upbringing as a result. Will Yamina's life come full circle with her past? Find out as Yasmina's crew, The Platinum Chicks, set out to make a name for themselves on the street.

In stores!!

Ashland's mother, Bianca, fights hard to suppress the truth from her daughter because she doesn't want her to marry Jordan, the grandson of an ex-lover she loathes. Ashland soon finds out how cruel and vengeful her mother can be, but what price will Bianca pay for redemption?

In stores!!

After Chasin' Satisfaction, Miko discovered that satisfaction is not all that it's cracked up to be. As a matter of fact, it left nothing but death in its aftermath. Now living the glamorous life in Miami while putting the finishing touches on his hybrid condo hotel, Julian realizes with newfound success he's now become the hunted.

Coming June 2009!!

An ex-drug dealer finds himself in a bind after he's caught by the Feds. He has to decide which is more important, his family or his loyalty to the game. As he fights hard to make a decision, those who helped him to the top fear the worse from him. Will he get the chance to tell the govt. whole story, or will someone get to him before he becomes a snitch?

In Stores!!

Malcolm is a wealthy virgin who decides to conceal his wealth From the world until he meets the right woman. His wealthy best friend, Dexter, hides his wealth from no one. Malcolm struggles to find love in an environment where vanity and materialism are rampant, while Dexter is getting more than enough of his share of women. Malcolm needs develop self-esteem and confidence to meet the right woman and Dexter's confidence is borderline arrogance.

Will bad boys like Dexter continue to take women for a ride?
Or will nice guys like Malcolm continue to finish last?

In Stores!!!

RICHARD JEANTY
Author of Neglected Souls and Neglected No More
INTRODUCES

WARNING
HIGHLY
ADDICTIVE
READING MATERIAL

Cater to Her

A NOVEL BY
SEAN MITCHELL

What happens when a woman's devotion to her fiancee is tested
weeks before she gets married? What if her fiancee is just hiding
behind the veil of ministry to deceive her? Find out as Sean Mitchell
takes you on a journey you'll never forget into the lives of Angelica,
Titus and Aurelius.

In Stores!!

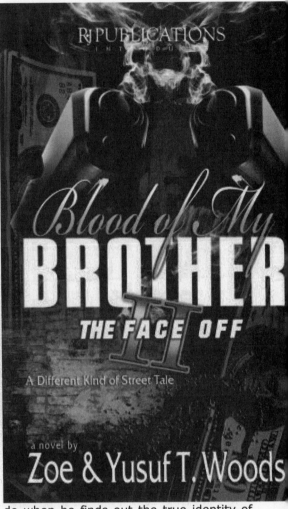

What will Roc do when he finds out the true identity of Solo? Will the blood shed come from his own brother Lil Mac? Will Roc and Solo take their beef to an explosive height on the street? Find out as Zoe and Yusuf bring the second installment to their hot street joint, Blood of My Brother.

In Stores!!

When an Ex-con finds himself destitute and in dire need of the basic necessities after he's released from prison, he turns to what he knows best, crime, but at what cost? Extortion, murder and mayhem drives him back to the top, but will he stay there?

In Stores!!

Successful investment tycoon Jack Anderson seems to have it all, success, money, charisma, good looks, even sex appeal. He might just be too good to be true. Will Rain Hunter find happiness in the arms of Jack, or is he just one more headache to add to her life? Find out as Cereka Cook takes you on a roller coaster ride in her new novel.

In Stores May 2009!!

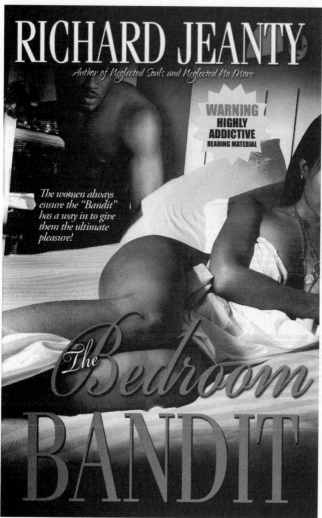

It may not be Histeria Lane, but these desperate housewives are fed up with their neglecting husbands. Their sexual needs take precedence over the millions of dollars their husbands bring home every year. While their husbands claim to be hard at work, these wives are doing a little work of their own with the bedroom bandit. Is the bandit swift enough to evade these angry husbands?

In Stores!!

PUBLICATIONS
BRINGING EXCITEMENT, FUN AND JOY TO READING

Use this coupon to order by mail

1. Neglected Souls, Richard Jeanty ($14.95) Available
2. Neglected No More, Richard Jeanty (-$14.95)Available
3. Sexual Exploits of Nympho, Richard Jeanty (-$14.95)
4. Meeting Ms. Right(Whip Appeal), Richard Jeanty ($14.95) Available
5. Me and Mrs. Jones, K.M Thompson ($14.95) Available
6. Chasin' Satisfaction, W.S Burkett ($14.95) Available
7. Extreme Circumstances, Cereka Cook ($14.95) Available
8. The Most Dangerous Gang In America, The NYPD, R. Jeanty ($15.00) Available
9. Sexual Exploits of a Nympho II, Richard Jeanty ($15.00) Available
10. Sexual Jeopardy, Richard Jeanty ($14.95) Coming: February 15, 2008
11. Too Many Secrets, Too Many Lies, Sonya Sparks ($15.00) Available
12. Stick And Move, Shawn Black ($15.00) Coming: January 15, 2008
13. Evil Side Of Money, Jeff Robertson ($15.00) Available
14. Cater To Her, W.S Burkett ($15.00) Coming March 2008
15. Blood of my Brother, Zoe & Ysuf Woods ($15.00) Available
16. Hoodfellas, Richard Jeanty ($15.00) November 2008
17. The Bedroom Bandit, Richard Jeanty ($15) January 2009

Name_____
Address_____
City_____State_____Zip Code_____

Please send the novels that I have circled above.

Shipping and Handling $1.99
Total Number of Books_____
Total Amount Due_____

This offer is subject to change without notice.
Send Bank check or money order (no cash or CODs) to:

RJ Publications
P.O. Box 300771
Jamaica, NY 11430

For more information please call 718-471-2926, or visit www.rjpublications.com

Please allow 2-3 weeks for delivery.

PUBLICATIONS
BRINGING EXCITEMENT, FUN AND JOY TO READING

Use this coupon to order by mail

18. Neglected Souls, Richard Jeanty ($14.95) Available
19. Neglected No More, Richard Jeanty (-$14.95)Available
20. Sexual Exploits of Nympho, Richard Jeanty (-$14.95)
21. Meeting Ms. Right(Whip Appeal), Richard Jeanty ($14.95) Available
22. Me and Mrs. Jones, K.M Thompson ($14.95) Available
23. Chasin' Satisfaction, W.S Burkett ($14.95) Available
24. Extreme Circumstances, Cereka Cook ($14.95) Available
25. The Most Dangerous Gang In America, The NYPD, R. Jeanty ($15.00) Available
26. Sexual Exploits of a Nympho II, Richard Jeanty ($15.00) Available
27. Sexual Jeopardy, Richard Jeanty ($14.95) Coming: February 15, 2008
28. Too Many Secrets, Too Many Lies, Sonya Sparks ($15.00) Available
29. Stick And Move, Shawn Black ($15.00) Coming: January 15, 2008
30. Evil Side Of Money, Jeff Robertson ($15.00) Available
31. Cater To Her, W.S Burkett ($15.00) Coming March 2008
32. Blood of my Brother, Zoe & Ysuf Woods ($15.00) Available
33. Hoodfellas, Richard Jeanty ($15.00) November 2008
34. The Bedroom Bandit, Richard Jeanty ($15) January 2009

Name_____
Address_____
City_____State_____Zip Code_____

Please send the novels that I have circled above.

Shipping and Handling $1.99
Total Number of Books_____
Total Amount Due_____

This offer is subject to change without notice.
Send Bank check or money order (no cash or CODs) to:

RJ Publications
P.O. Box 300771
Jamaica, NY 11430

For more information please call 718-471-2926, or visit www.rjpublications.com

Please allow 2-3 weeks for delivery.

PUBLICATIONS
BRINGING EXCITEMENT, FUN AND JOY TO READING

Use this coupon to order by mail

35. Neglected Souls, Richard Jeanty ($14.95) Available
36. Neglected No More, Richard Jeanty (-$14.95)Available
37. Sexual Exploits of Nympho, Richard Jeanty (-$14.95)
38. Meeting Ms. Right(Whip Appeal), Richard Jeanty ($14.95) Available
39. Me and Mrs. Jones, K.M Thompson ($14.95) Available
40. Chasin' Satisfaction, W.S Burkett ($14.95) Available
41. Extreme Circumstances, Cereka Cook ($14.95) Available
42. The Most Dangerous Gang In America, The NYPD, R. Jeanty ($15.00) Available
43. Sexual Exploits of a Nympho II, Richard Jeanty ($15.00) Available
44. Sexual Jeopardy, Richard Jeanty ($14.95) Coming: February 15, 2008
45. Too Many Secrets, Too Many Lies, Sonya Sparks ($15.00) Available
46. Stick And Move, Shawn Black ($15.00) Coming: January 15, 2008
47. Evil Side Of Money, Jeff Robertson ($15.00) Available
48. Cater To Her, W.S Burkett ($15.00) Coming March 2008
49. Blood of my Brother, Zoe & Ysuf Woods ($15.00) Available
50. Hoodfellas, Richard Jeanty ($15.00) November 2008
51. The Bedroom Bandit, Richard Jeanty ($15) January 2009

Name_____

Address_____

City_____State_____Zip Code_____

Please send the novels that I have circled above.

Shipping and Handling $1.99

Total Number of Books_____

Total Amount Due_____

This offer is subject to change without notice.
Send Bank check or money order (no cash or CODs) to:

RJ Publications
P.O. Box 300771
Jamaica, NY 11430

For more information please call 718-471-2926, or visit www.rjpublications.com

Please allow 2-3 weeks for delivery.